The
STAR-SPANGLED
BANNER

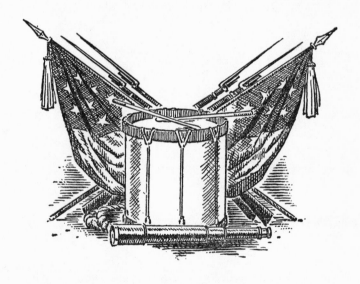

The
STAR-SPANGLED
BANNER

The Thrilling Story of a Boy
Who Lived the Words
of Our National Anthem

By NEIL H. SWANSON

and ANNE SHERBOURNE SWANSON

Illustrated by Norman Guthrie Rudolph

HOLT, RINEHART and WINSTON
New York · Chicago · San Francisco

2360

In Canada, Holt, Rinehart and Winston
of Canada, Limited

Library of Congress Catalogue Card Number: 58-5675

Published, April, 1958
Second printing, November, 1962
Third printing, February, 1965
Fourth printing, March, 1966
Fifth printing, January, 1967

F
Swa

98251-0212
PRINTED IN THE UNITED STATES OF AMERICA

FOR JOHN AND LITTLE ANNE

Books by the Authors

By Neil H. Swanson
and Anne Sherbourne Swanson
The Star-Spangled Banner

By Neil H. Swanson
Unconquered
The Perilous Fight
The Silent Drum
The Forbidden Ground
The First Rebel
The Phantom Emperor
The Judas Tree
The Flag Is Still There

About the Authors

NEIL H. SWANSON is a leading authority on the exciting and important events that led to the writing of our national anthem in September, 1814. His work in that field has brought him a number of outstanding honors bestowed by the various War of 1812 societies. He has served five terms as president of the Star-Spangled Banner Flag House Association, guardian of the house in which was made the huge battle flag that inspired Francis Scott Key. The Flag House is the only patriotic shrine in the United States where both the Stars and Stripes of today, and the fifteen-star, fifteen-stripe flag of 1812 fly day and night by special permission of Congress.

Mr. Swanson was born in Minneapolis, Minnesota, and is a graduate of the university of that state. He was in the Army during World War I, and upon his return from overseas, he embarked upon a successful newspaper career. After serving in executive capacities for newspapers in Minneapolis, Pittsburgh, and Baltimore, he retired from the news world to devote all his time to research, writing, and public speaking. Thus far, as novelist and historian, he can claim seven best sellers.

In the interests of research, he has traveled hundreds of thousands of miles all over the world. One of the most unusual experiences resulting from these journeys was getting his shoes burned off while climbing Vesuvius to photograph a crater during eruption.

Anne Sherbourne Swanson was born in Baltimore,

Maryland and attended schools there. While still in her teens, she was listed in *Who's Who in America* as a newspaper columnist, and radio and television commentator. She was a columnist with by-line for newspapers in Washington, Baltimore, and Philadelphia, and later did public relations and publicity for a leading Philadelphia department store. Currently a busy expert in fashion advertising, she finds time to collaborate on literary projects with her husband, write books of her own, and attend to the upbringing of her two children at home in Garrison, Maryland.

THE STAR-SPANGLED BANNER is the first book the Swansons have written together, but they have been a successful writing and research team for many years. They feel that this is one of the few books ever written for young people which gives an accurate picture of the days in which the national anthem was born. They consider the action at Fort McHenry one of the decisive battles of our history and hope that inspiration may be drawn from true knowledge of the courage displayed during those desperate days—days which, in their minds, made the United States a nation.

Contents

Forgotten Heroes

We Americans are fond of heroes.

We write books about them, give them medals, carve their names on monuments.

The lives of those to whom the names belonged are mingled with our lives. For they are a part of the country they helped to build, and we too are a part of our country.

This book is a story about heroes, but it is a little different from most such books. These heroes are not famous. They were given no medals. So . . .

This is a story of courage that America forgot—a story of brave men and boys whose names you have never heard.

Quite probably, you have never heard of the dangers they faced and the battles they fought to save this country of ours.

It is hard to realize, now, that the President of the United States was once driven out of Washington by an invading army.

He fled on horseback into a stormy night. Foreign soldiers pillaged and burned the White House.

The date was August 24, in 1814.

Nearly forty years had gone by since the Declaration of Independence was signed. But the United States was fighting again for its life.

It is hard to realize, now, that the Declaration itself was saved that night by being stuffed into a sack and carried away in a farmer's wagon.

It is hard to realize, now, that many Americans believed

xiii

that the war was lost—and, with it, the independence of the United States. Many Englishmen, too, believed that our country would soon be, again, only a British colony.

Eighteen days after the burning of Washington, the same foreign army and a powerful foreign fleet attacked Baltimore. During the three-day battle that ended in British defeat, a young American artillery lieutenant— a prisoner in the attacking fleet—anxiously watched the flag that flew over a small red-brick fort.

On the third morning he saw, by the dawn's early light, the fifteen bright stars and the fifteen broad stripes streaming out through the smoke and flame that engulfed the fort.

The bombardment roared on. The battle was not yet over. The outcome was still in doubt. But Lt. Francis Scott Key pulled an envelope out of his pocket and started to scribble the words of a song.

It wasn't a song of triumph and victory. All day, all night, and the half of another day would go by before any American could be sure that victory had been won.

It was a song of defiance. It was a song of courage and hope and endurance. It was a song of brave men whose bodies stood as a living rampart between their loved homes and the foe who had come to destroy them.

The song was "The Star-Spangled Banner."

Wouldn't you think that those desperate days, which gave us our national anthem, would make one of the most thrilling chapters in the story of our country? They don't. The strangest thing in the whole written history of the United States is its failure to tell the truth about those days.

For more than 140 years, the Battle of Baltimore has

been falsely described as "an event of no importance"—
as "a trifling skirmish"—and as "a disgraceful affair" in
which the "cowardly" Americans "ran like rabbits."

Well, the rabbits are in this book. Follow Lex Landon,
as Lex tried to follow his father to war, and you will see
them just as they were . . . young Dan Wells and Henry
McComas . . . Greg Andre . . . Sergeant MacKensie . . .
John Montgomery . . . Dr. Sam Martin . . . Josh Batchelor,
who carried the flag that his father had carried at Cowpens . . . and the old man who went down fighting to save
the guns.

You can decide for yourself what kind of rabbits they
were.

You can decide for yourself whether being forgotten
was all the reward they deserved.

THE AUTHORS

Chapter 1

A BOY GOES HUNTING FOR A WAR

THE boy stopped running when he saw the cannon in the street ahead of him.

It was upside down.

Both wheels were in the air.

Its brass barrel was half buried in the deep, soft dust.

The ammunition box lay smashed against a tree. One end was split into pieces. Through the splintered wood, the boy could see the rows of gray-cloth cartridges inside. Some of them had been ripped open. He could see black cannon powder spilling out of the torn places.

There was something frightening about that wrecked gun, lying in the empty street in Washington.

It told Lex Landon that he was too late. It told him that the battle was all over. But it couldn't tell him what had happened to his father.

1

The boy shivered.

He was hot and panting after his long run through the silent city, all the way from the Potomac River to this hilltop within plain sight of the house where the President of the United States lived.

Big drops of sweat swelled on his forehead like the welts of bee stings. The blobs trickled down his face in crooked streaks.

His clothes were soaking wet. His pantaloons were gummy with the dust that covered him. His linen shirt was sticking to his skin. Where the flintlock musket lay across his shoulder, the yellow dust had turned to mud.

The air he breathed felt like the blast of heat that came out when his mother opened the iron door of the Dutch oven in the kitchen chimney place, back home in Alexandria.

But he was cold with fear.

He knew that the Americans had fought the British Army somewhere up in Maryland this afternoon of August 24 in 1814. He had heard the guns! They were a long way off, across the river from the Virginia town where Lex Landon lived. The noise they made was like the jolting of a wagon over the loose planks of a bridge. It was a kind of hollow bump . . . bump! Then a long wait. And then brr-rump . . . bump . . . brump!

That was when Lex started to get scared. His father would be in the battle, and he'd be on horseback. He would be a target, with his red sash and his sword and the gold fringe of a major on the shoulders of his blue coat. Every dull brump! of the cannon might mean that he had been killed.

Lex couldn't stand it. He couldn't stay at home, just

listening and worrying and waiting. He knew his mother wouldn't let him go. So he had slipped away without telling her good-by. He had come up the Potomac River in his log sail canoe to Washington, to try to find out whether the Americans were winning.

And then, while he was in the middle of the river, the distant bumping of the guns had stopped. That had been hours ago, but he didn't know, yet, how the battle had turned out.

Lex Landon was too big to be afraid. He was only an inch shorter than the musket on his shoulder. He was fourteen years old, going three months onto fifteen. Next year, if the United States was still at war with England, he'd be in the army.

A boy who was almost a soldier shouldn't be afraid.

But Lex was shaking, now. He couldn't help it. The cold shivers wouldn't stop. They made him feel ashamed.

He was still staring at the overturned brass cannon when a sudden sound cracked like a rifleshot. His head jerked around.

A painted coach was coming down the driveway from the big house that some people called the President's Palace and some people called the White House.

Lex saw the driver raise his arm. His long whip cracked again. The horses flattened themselves and began to run. Dust boiled up around them.

The coach swung into the wide street. It leaned far over as it made the turn. It swayed from one side to the other on its leather slings. Three or four men followed it on horseback.

Lex jumped out of the way as they rushed by.

Watching the coach and the little group of riders was

like seeing ghosts in daylight. The hoofs of horses running ought to make a noise like thunder, or at least like drums. They didn't, though. They made hardly any noise at all in the thick dust. The men behind were only dim blurs in the blinding cloud that whirled up from the wheels.

Lex didn't know that Mrs. Madison, the President's wife, was in that bouncing coach.

But he knew, now, that the Americans had lost the battle.

That was why the city was so quiet and so empty. That was why the windows of the shops were boarded up, and why the shutters of the houses were closed tight.

Something terrible had happened—something worse than a lost battle.

The army sent out to defend this fine new Capital of the United States had run away.

It had still been running when it came back to Washington again, miles from the place where it had fought the British. And it hadn't stopped. It hadn't even tried to save the city. It was trying to escape. Only soldiers who were in a panic would have left that cannon lying in the street.

The British Army must be close behind them.

Lex had heard dreadful stories about how the British acted when they captured an American town. They had plundered Hampton, on the James River in Virginia. They had burned Havre de Grace and Fredericktown and Georgetown, up in Maryland. For more than a year, their warships had been swarming in Chesapeake Bay, and their marines and sailors had been raiding the plantations and the villages along the shore.

Some people said that they behaved like Indians,

attacking helpless towns at night, setting fire to houses, and then dancing in the red glare of the flames.

Now they must be coming to burn Washington.

Lex knew that he ought not to be here. He ought to get away before it was too late.

But he didn't move. He felt as if he couldn't. He was numb with a new kind of fear. When the British came to Washington, they would see the roofs of Alexandria on the other side of the Potomac. They could cross the river on the long bridge. In a few hours, his own home might be burning.

He thought about his mother and his sister Robin. They ought not to stay in Alexandria. He ought to warn them that the enemy was coming. Then he thought about his father. Major Landon might be lying by the roadside somewhere, wounded.

Lex made up his mind. He couldn't go back home until he had found out about his father. Maybe he was doing wrong, but he was going to follow the retreating army.

He had taken only two steps when a team of horses came out of an alley. They had harness on their backs, and long, iron trace chains were dragging behind them. The chains plowed crooked furrows in the dirt.

An old man was leading the two horses—a man so thin, so bent, so leathery and dried up, that he looked like a worn-out wagon whip. His face was a nest of wrinkles. Even the top of his bald head was wrinkled.

He was not a soldier. Anyway, he wasn't dressed like one. He wore a checkered shirt and ragged overalls. But he led the horses to the cannon and turned the animals around, and then backed them toward one of the wheels that stuck up in the air.

Suddenly he yelled at Lex: "You! You, there! What you doin' with that musket?" His voice was as squeaky as a rusty hinge, but it was hard, too, the way an iron hinge would be underneath the rust. "Come over here an' help me. Grab ahold of these here bridles! An' be quick about it. You act like you *wanted* this here cannon to be lyin' handy for the Britishers to capture. Do you? *Speak up!* Do you?"

"No, sir."

"Then git a move on! Don't just stand there gawpin' at me. Hold these horses while I git a trace chain hooked around a wheel."

Lex walked slowly to the horses' heads. He let the musket slide down through his slippery hands, until the butt sank deep into the dust. He leaned the muzzle on his chest so he could use both hands to grip the bridles.

The little old man scuttled around behind the team and picked up one of the chains. The links clanked and rattled on the cannon wheel. The rusty voice squeaked again:

"Now we're gittin' somewhere. Hold 'em steady. What's your name, bub?"

"Lex."

"That ain't much of a name. Ain't you got no more names?"

"Yes." Lex was getting angry. This ragged, dirty, withered-up old man was making fun of his name. "It's Alexander Hamilton Landon."

"That's quite a mouthful of a name. You probably ain't worth it. Boy that's got a name like that ought not to be as scairt as you are. Back those horses up, Lex.

Easy . . . easy. . . . That's it. Any minute now the Britishers will be acomin' up this street."

"They . . . they . . ." Lex Landon's hands were shaking on the bridles, and his voice was shaking. "They won the battle, didn't they?"

"I dunno as you could say it was a battle. But we're licked, boy. We're licked bad."

"The army . . ." Lex was stammering. "Where's our army?"

"Army!" All the wrinkles in the withered old face pulled together in a kind of knot. "We ain't got no army!"

"But our men! What happened to our men? They're not all . . . ?"

"No, bub. They ain't killed or wounded. A few of 'em, maybe. But not many. They were runnin' too fast for a musket ball to catch 'em."

"My father wouldn't run!" Lex's face was white with both fear and anger. "He was in the Revolution."

"That so? Well, then, he sure did his share of runnin'."

"He did not! He was at Trenton!" That was how Lex got his name. He had been named for Capt. Alexander Hamilton. His father had been a gunner in Captain Hamilton's artillery company when Washington's army crossed the Delaware and fought the British in a snowstorm.

"Ain't your dad never told you how we ran at Trenton?"

"We didn't run! We whipped them!"

"Sure we whipped 'em. At first. That's the part that folks remember. But a lot more of the redcoats came, an'

we sneaked off in the dark. That's what we mostly did.
Six years of runnin', Lex. Six years of sneakin' off an'
dodgin'. Long Island, Chad's Ford, Germantown. . . ."
The iron hook at the end of the harness chain grated
into one of the links. "An' a lot of little battles you ain't
never heard of, likely, an' we ran away from all of 'em.
Now, boy, you lead those horses ahead, slow. *Slow*, I
said!"

The chain tightened. The cannon groaned and tilted.
The wheel came down with a hard bump.

"There! We're agoin' to do it, Lex. The United States
ain't got no army, but it's still got you an' me. The
Britishers think they can walk right into Washington.
But we're agoin' to show 'em, bub. Yes, sir!"

It sounded crazy. What could one old man and one
boy do against an army? Yet the rickety little man came
hurrying to take the horses' bridles.

"You an' me will show 'em! When you an' me an' this
old cannon open up on 'em, they'll be surprised worse
than they were at Trenton. You know what a linstock is,
boy?"

"Yes," Lex said. "My father was a gunner."

"That so? What you say his name is?"

"Major Thomas Landon."

"Major, eh?" He didn't sound as if he thought a major
was important. "You go fetch a linstock out of that there
powder chest. Fetch the tinderbox, too. You git that
linstock burnin' while I haul this gun out of the gutter.
We're agoin' to put this cannon smack-dab in the middle
of the street, an' when the Britishers show up . . ."

"There they come now!" Lex cried.

A scarlet column was turning into the street, less than

a quarter of a mile away. A haze of dust hung over it, but the setting sun gleamed on the polished musket barrels and the long, sharp bayonets.

"Grits an' gravy! We ain't got no time to load this cannon. Look ahere, boy. What you got in that there popgun?"

"Three buckshot and a ball," Lex said.

"Fine! That's fine, bub!" The skinny hands let go of the bridles and snatched up the musket. "I've fought the Britishers three times. I don't mean just three battles, neither. I mean three diff'rent times. I fought 'em up in Pennsylvania in 1765, ten years before the Revolution, an' I helped to lick 'em. Most folks have forgotten, but we took a fort away from 'em. Fort Loudon, its name was. Four years after that, we took another fort away from 'em. There was only twenty of us, but we rushed Fort Bedford an' we took it, six years before Ethan Allen took Ticonderoga. Yes, sir! We licked the British regulars! We licked the Royal Irish—redcoats out of the same regiment that was at Lexington an' Concord. We licked the Black Watch that was at Long Island. An' I fought 'em again in the Revolution, all the way from Boston down to Yorktown. We had an army then, boy. That old Continental Army was a tough one. We ran, when we had to, but we came back. We kept comin' back until they hollered quits. An' then today . . ."

The wrinkled face puckered up. The old man looked as if he felt like crying.

"You know what they did to me today, boy?"

"No, sir." The British troops were getting closer. Lex could see the shine of buckles on the white crossbelts of the front rank.

"Our own army said I was too old to fight. That's what the off'cers said. I ain't but ninety-two years old, but they wouldn't let me into the militia. The fools! That's what they are—fools! But I got the last laugh on 'em. Our whole army's run away, but old Joe Piery is still here to fight the Britishers. I'll get one more shot at 'em, by glory!"

The old man was laughing. To Lex, it sounded like his sister Robin giggling when she knew that she was getting into mischief.

"Boy, you're agoin' to see somethin' you'll remember. You see those two off'cers there, on horseback? That one in the red coat is the gen'ral. An' the one alongside of him, in the blue coat—he's a naval off'cer. Might be he's an admiral. Yes, sir. Might be he's the off'cer that's been settin' fire to people's houses all along the Chesapeake this summer. Co'burn, I mean. You've heard tell about him, ain't you?"

"Yes." Lex could see the officers on horseback plainly —much too plainly. It wasn't sensible to stand here, talking, talking.

"Now, bub," the old man said, "you start makin' tracks. We ain't got but one gun, an' there ain't a mite of use for both of us to stay here. Don't you be ashamed of runnin'. When you see your dad, you ask him does he recollect Joe Piery. Ask him if we didn't sneak away at Trenton. Your dad an' I were workin' the same cannon. I was a full-growed man, an' Tom Landon wasn't an inch taller than you are this minute. But he wasn't no more scairt than I was. If he ran today, it was because there wasn't nothin' else he *could* do."

Joe Piery hooked his thumb around the lock of Lex's musket. It clicked as he pulled it back.

"Git out of here," he said. "Don't you let 'em redcoats catch you. They ain't agoin' to like it when I fire your popgun at 'em. You run faster 'n ever you ran in your life, boy. That's an order. Git!"

Chapter 2

TRAPPED IN A HOUSE
THAT SMELLS OF SMOKE

LEX turned and ran. When he looked back across his shoulder, the old man was gone.

The horses stood there by themselves, still harnessed to the brass gun. Behind them, the red-coated column filled the street from side to side.

The British troops were marching at attention, keeping step. All of their black-leather helmets bobbed together. All of their bright jackets swayed at the same time.

A strange thought flashed into Lex's mind: They don't look like men. The long column looked like something crawling. It looked like a huge snake, swallowing the street.

Lex ran with all his might. At every step, he listened for a shot.

If Joe Piery fired into those scarlet ranks, the soldiers would shoot back. They'd surely shoot at anybody they saw trying to get away.

Maybe it would have been better not to run. Soldiers wouldn't shoot a boy, just standing still and watching them. Or would they?

Lex didn't know, but he knew that this broad, empty street was a bad place to be. There were fences on both sides of it. They penned him in.

One of them was a blank wall of boards nailed close together. It was higher than his head. He couldn't climb it.

The other was a yellow picket fence, and all the palings had sharp, pointed tops. They, too, were higher than his head. But there was a gate between two tall square posts. Behind the gate, there was a big front yard, and then a yellow house with big square pillars and steps going up between them to a porch.

The windows of the house weren't hidden behind shutters. Maybe there were people in it. Maybe they would let him in and hide him.

He ran toward the gate. It was chained shut, and the chain was fastened with a padlock.

Lex looked for a toehold in the yellow gate. There wasn't any. The cracks between the palings were too narrow. The chain! If he could get one foot into that loop of chain . . . !

He reached up and took hold of the sharp tops of two palings. He lifted himself by his arms and tried to find the chain with one foot. The toe of his shoe touched it, but it slipped away.

As he hung there, panting, he could see the cannon.

And then, suddenly, he couldn't see it! The front ranks of the marching redcoats opened. They split neatly in the middle and became two columns, one on each side of the cannon. When they passed the team, they joined again into one solid mass.

Lex shuddered. It seemed to him as if huge jaws had opened wide and swallowed both the brass gun and the horses.

His foot found the chain again. His toe wriggled into the loop. There! If he could lift himself a little higher, he could jump.

He held on with one hand and grabbed for the gate-post with the other. The chain made a kind of stirrup. He could stand up in it. He was putting his other foot into the V-shaped space between two pointed pickets when he heard the musket go off.

It was his gun. He knew how it sounded—sharper than an army musket. That crazy old man! Fighting the whole British Army, all alone! Joe Piery *must* be crazy. Or else braver than most other men—a whole lot braver than Lex Landon felt right now.

Lex wanted to jump, but he couldn't. The chain was twisted tight around his foot.

The soldiers had stopped marching. A little way back in the column, the two mounted officers were sitting on their horses, motionless.

Finally, one of them began to move—the one in the red coat. He seemed to be getting taller. He was being lifted higher than the officer in the blue coat, beside him. His gray horse was rearing—but not fast, the way a horse did when it was excited. It rose slowly on its hind legs. Higher . . . higher. . . . It went over backward.

As it fell, the rider sprang off. The horse lay on its side. Its legs moved as if it were walking. Then they stopped.

The officer in the blue coat was shouting. He waved his arm and pointed. Red-coated officers on foot began to shout, too. Their swords flashed. It seemed to Lex that the blades were pointing in a dozen different directions.

Groups of soldiers broke off from the column. A whole platoon of them ran toward the frame house at the corner, where he had first seen the skinny old man leading the two horses. As the soldiers ran, they spread out. They were trying to surround Joe Piery, but that wasn't all. Two smaller groups were coming down both sides of this wide street. They were hunting for *him,* too.

Lex jerked frantically at his foot. The shoe came off. He jumped.

It wasn't a good jump. It was a headlong dive. The ground came up and hit him in the chest.

He lay there and looked at the yellow house—and what he saw behind the windows hit him harder than the packed dirt of the driveway. There were shutters on the inside, and they were closed tight. He knew, now, why the gate was padlocked. This house, too, had been deserted.

Lex got up on his hands and knees. He looked around him wildly. In the whole bare yard, there was no place to hide. His only chance was to get around the corner of the house before the soldiers reached the fence and saw him through the pickets.

He took one step—and felt the gravel gouging through his stocking. His shoe! If the soldiers saw it hanging in the chain, they'd know somebody had climbed over the high gate.

Turning back to that gate was the hardest thing he'd ever done. He forced himself to do it. When he peeped through one of the thin cracks, the shoe wasn't where it had been. It had come loose when he pulled his foot out. It was lying on the ground outside the gate.

Lex went down in the driveway, on his stomach, and reached underneath and got it. As he pulled it toward him, he could hear the soldiers yelling:

"Two of 'em . . . nah, more 'n that . . . ten . . . tellin' ye, I saw 'em . . . dirty Yankees. . . ." The yells were jerky with the soldiers' running. ". . . cowards, they are . . . hidin' . . . general's horse . . . could have been him. . . ."

Lex's hands were shaking, but he made himself take time to pull his other shoe off. Then he ran, with one shoe in each hand.

He passed a slanting cellar door—and that was pad-locked, too. More windows—and more shutters on the inside, and all of them closed. The back corner of the house was just ahead. If he could get that far before they saw him . . . ! With the house between him and the street, he'd have half a minute more to find a place to hide. There had to be some place. There *had* to be!

He turned the corner. The back door was standing open!

He could not believe it. People wouldn't close a house up tight, and then forget a door. They might, he thought. If they were scared, they might. Hadn't he almost forgotten his own shoe?

The soldiers were at the gate, now. The chain rattled as they tried it. A hoarse voice bawled:

"Blow it off!"

A musket slammed. He heard wood splintering, and then a rush of boots along the driveway. They were coming after him!

He stepped through the doorway into a dim room that smelled of fried potatoes.

Instantly, he wished he hadn't done it. Blows thundered on the front door. The house boomed with echoes. He knew, now, that the soldiers hadn't seen him. If they had, they wouldn't waste time beating on the front door. He should have kept on running.

It was too late to change his mind. Some of the soldiers were clattering down the porch steps. Their feet were thudding on the lawn. If he'd ever had a chance to get away, he'd lost it.

Lex closed the door. The key was on the inside. He set his shoes down on the floor. He wrapped the fingers of one hand around the long shank of the key and used the other hand to twist it, slowly, so it wouldn't rattle. When the door was locked, he pulled the key out.

I'm not scared, he told himself. I'm *not*. I remembered to take out the key. I remembered that if they should try to look in through the keyhole, and the key was in it, they'd know the door was locked from the inside. If all the other doors are locked from the inside, they'd know somebody's in the house. They can't be sure, now.

Lex stood in the dark, trying to remember how the kitchen looked before he closed the door. A brick fireplace, with iron kettles hanging on a crane. A stairway in one corner. A table somewhere, but he wasn't sure where. There had been dishes on it—and a red cloth—and knives and forks and spoons stuck into tall glass tumblers.

If he bumped into that table . . . Just the thought of a

dish falling on the floor and breaking was enough to make cold prickles run along his arms. He'd have to use both hands to feel his way.

He unbuttoned the top buttons of his shirt, picked up his shoes and pushed them in against his chest, and buttoned the shirt over them. Then, bending over so his hands were lower than a table top would be, he moved slowly toward the corner where the stairs were.

He didn't lift his feet; he slid them. The kitchen must be bigger than he'd thought. It seemed to take hours, crossing it. The next thing he knew, his hands touched the stairs. He'd missed the table altogether.

The stairs were narrow. They climbed steeply into greater darkness. The air grew hotter, but the sound of battering on the front door grew fainter.

He was halfway up when he heard a noise below him— knuckles on the back door—a boot kicking at it. Every second, he expected to hear gun butts smashing in the panels.

Suddenly the stairway ended. A streak of light showed underneath a door. He opened it. Hot air gushed out to meet him. He was standing at the bottom of another flight of stairs, still narrower and steeper. At the top, a tiny window glistened. Its four panes were red with sunset.

That's queer, Lex thought. That isn't west. It's north. It ought to be. Already, in this strange house, he was getting mixed up.

He was four steps from the top when he saw that he was not mixed up. The red sheen on the four small panes was not the sunset. It was fire.

He was looking down at the frame house on the corner. There were soldiers all around it, and the house was burning. Flames curled out of broken windows. They licked upward to the eaves and nibbled at the edges of the shingles.

Lex saw soldiers picking up rocks in the street and throwing them to break more windows. He couldn't see Joe Piery anywhere. Had the old man got away? Or had the soldiers caught him? They weren't . . . ? Surely they weren't burning the house with Joe Piery in it?

Lex felt cold sweat breaking out on him like blisters. He knew that when the British attacked Havre de Grace, they'd shot flaming rockets at the town and set fire to houses while the people were still sleeping in them.

Smoke was seeping through the shingles of the frame house, now. As Lex watched, one front corner of the roof curled up. Black-red smoke and red-black flames came pouring out. The whole roof exploded. He could hear the crashing as it burst apart. No! No, he couldn't! The crash he heard was different. It wasn't out there, where the flames were leaping. It was in here! It was in this house.

He listened. For a moment, there was only the dull thudding of his own heart. Then there were other thuds. The redcoats were downstairs somewhere. And they were coming upstairs!

Lex was really scared, now. Hide . . . hide . . . I've got to hide!

There were four windows in the attic, one on each side. He could see three of them plainly. The fourth was almost hidden by a clutter of trunks, boxes, a child's high chair, an old ladder—all the things that people put away in attics.

Lex went down on his hands and knees. He squeezed

between a packing box and a trunk with iron bands around it. Behind them, the roof came almost to the floor—but the floor wasn't there. It stopped before it reached the eaves. The ends of the planks had been sawed off every which way. There was a space almost a foot deep between them and the ceiling lath below—a space wide enough for him to crawl between two of the joists. Lex crept into it, feet first, and wriggled backward until his head was underneath the floor.

He lay there, listening again. The soldiers were tramping through the second-floor hall. He could hear them talking—shouting, probably. But here in this hot hide-hole where he lay, their talk was only a dull blur of sound.

The window just in front of him was a dull blur, too. It was beginning to get dark. His mother would be worrying about him. In a little while, now, she'd be going to the front steps, looking for him down the cobbled slope toward the Potomac wharves. She'd be calling, "Robin! Robi-i-nn, have you seen Lex?"

Right now, likelier than not, that snub-nosed sister of his was dangling her bare feet from the top of a wharf piling, waiting for him. Or else she'd be perched out on the far end of the bowsprit of his father's schooner, with her scratched legs wrapped around it.

Thinking of the boat made tears come up behind his eyelids. The schooner was the *Lex and Robin*. It was named for both of them. Would he ever see it again? Would he ever see his mother and his sister—or his father? Would he ever know what happened to his father in the battle? Would his family ever know what happened to *him*?

The noise of tramping feet was louder. They were on the attic stairs—and Lex remembered that the stairs were dusty. He must have left a plain trail.

But there wasn't enough light for the soldiers to see footprints on the stairway. He heard a disgusted voice say: "Aghh, come along. There's quicker ways to catch a rabbit than settin' ferrets on him. Smoke him out, I say. Burn him out, the way they did the other." Another soldier said, "Ay, roasted rabbit." And then all of them were laughing.

Lex felt the shakes take hold of him again. The trembling started in his legs. It quivered all along his back and up into his shoulders. When it reached his throat, it was like swallowing the wrong way, and he couldn't stop.

He lay there for a long time, shaking, after the last sounds had gone away. The dark closed in on him.

He smelled the smoke. It stung his nose, and made his throat hurt with a tight, dry aching. He could even taste smoke—sour and spoiled and sickish.

It was pitch-dark in the attic—and outdoors, too. Lex couldn't see the window only an arm's length away. But he still kept seeing, in his mind, the fierce flames curling out of other windows, scorching the side of the frame house up the street. He kept seeing the roof torn loose and lifted—the whole roof floating for a moment on the ugly cloud of black smoke, and then falling back into the fire.

He was sure the air here in the attic was much hotter than it had been a few minutes ago. He was sure the soldiers had set fire to this house, too. Right now, they probably were all around it, waiting.

But if the house was burning, every second he stayed in it made his chances poorer. The steep, narrow halls enclosing the stairways would draw the fire like chimney flues.

He started to crawl over the hard, gritty ridges of the plaster that bulged up between the laths. It was like crawling over a grater. The sharp bulges scraped his knees. But he hooked his fingertips over first one lumpy ridge and then another, and used his arms to drag him· self ahead.

Now he was almost out from underneath the floor. The ends of the planks dug into his back when he raised himself on his braced arms, but he hardly noticed the new hurt. The window had winked at him!

He crouched, staring at the flicker of flame outside the little pane. It had been there—it was gone—it came back. It was bigger this time. It turned both the lower panes red. Then they were black again. He couldn't see them. Suddenly the whole window seemed to jump into the attic toward him. All four panes were red with fire.

Lex tried to swallow, and the hot, dry lining of his throat pulled tight and choked him. His eyes smarted. He felt something running down his cheeks. I'm not crying! I'm not! But he had to dig his knuckles into his eyes, hard, to see the window. The knuckles came away wet. He pressed his face against the glass.

There was a big fire across the river—the worst fire he'd ever seen. It was shooting higher than the tops of tall trees. The flames themselves looked like enormous trees, with a storm bending them and tossing their long limbs.

He could see the bridge that led from Washington to

the Virginia shore. The southern end of it was blazing furiously.

The red light was growing brighter. It was climbing higher . . . higher. The dark night was turning swiftly into a strange, awful daylight.

Every moment, Lex could see more of the city spreading out below him—first the tallest chimneys, and then patches of woods with dark gullies of streets running through them, and then roofs of houses. He could see the vacant lots and backyards—sheds and fences—and finally the streets themselves, going up and down the low hills toward the river.

He looked downstream—and gasped. The navy yard was burning!

The flames there didn't look like trees. They made a wide, flat sheet of fire that seemed to be suspended from the sky. It hung there, flapping slowly, like a wet red tablecloth pinned to a clothesline. When it moved, Lex saw the masts of warships.

Lex knew that tears were running down his face. He didn't care. Those beautiful, tall ships! He'd seen them as he came upriver, only a few hours ago. One of them was the big new frigate *Essex,* the finest warship that the United States had ever built. It would never fight, now.

He wasn't crying because he was frightened for himself. He was frightened for his country. It was young and weak, and it was fighting all alone against the strongest nation in the world. It was like Joe Piery, trying to stand up to the whole British Army.

"We're licked," Joe Piery'd said. "Licked bad." It must be true. It must be, when the enemy could walk into the Capital of the United States and burn its ships.

Lex didn't know that the Americans themselves had set fire to the navy buildings and the dockyard. He was sure the British troops had done it. He was sure, now, that they were burning the whole city!

The glare outside was lighting up the attic. He could see that one window was open a few inches at the bottom, and smoke was drifting in. Maybe this house wasn't burning. Maybe there weren't any soldiers outside, waiting. . . .

He crept down the steep stairs. The long hall on the second floor was darker than the attic. But he saw a stair rail slanting downward, and white banisters with red light licking at them. When he came close enough to look between them, he could see the front door, splintered and wrenched from its hinges, lying on the floor below.

Lex wanted to get out! And he could get out quicker if he slid. He threw one leg across the rail and let himself go.

The banisters began to curve. Even while he was still sliding, he twisted himself sideways. He dropped without knowing what was underneath him, sprawled on the broken door, and felt a splinter drive into his palm.

He jerked his hand and heard the sound of thin wood breaking. But his hand was loose. And the front yard was empty! There weren't any soldiers waiting for him!

Lex lunged through the doorway into a sight more terrible than any nightmare.

Chapter 3

A PILLAR OF FIRE BY NIGHT

A GREAT arch of fierce light curved above the city. One end of it was out in the Potomac, and the other end was on the wooded hills along the south edge of the town.

It made Lex think of an enormous rainbow, burning.

To the right, the sheet of fire still hung down from the sky above the navy yard. In front of him—and closer— the big building where the Congress met was burning. Nearer yet, the President's house was spouting flames. They curved out from the windows and up over the high eaves, and joined together in one slender, towering flame that climbed and climbed up toward the fiery rainbow. The column of fire reminded Lex of something in the Bible.

The pillar of fire by night, he thought. I know now how it looked.

25

But this wasn't a pillar made by God to guide frightened people and help them to escape from enemies who were pursuing them. Or was it? No! No, surely not. It wasn't right to have such thoughts. It was wrong and silly to be thinking that the President's own house was burning to help one frightened boy escape.

But this pillar of fire was showing him which way to go. It was showing him a turnstile in the yellow fence along the side of the big yard. It was showing him a field beyond the stile, and a path almost hidden by tall rose of Sharon bushes matted thick with honeysuckle. He could see the path sloping down into a deep ravine, and, farther on, the ravine itself disappearing into a dark clump of woods.

Lex ran to the end of the porch, put both hands on the broad rail, and jumped. His feet came down into the lumpy dry dirt of a flower bed. The clods crumbled under his weight. Then the brittle, dry grass of the lawn was prickling through his stockings.

His hand touched the turnstile. It spun easily, without a sound. His feet were on the smoothness of the path, and the path was taking him down into the ravine. The banks rose higher than his head. The laced branches of big oaks and honey locusts made a kind of roof above him.

The glare of fire came through the thick tops of the trees in speckles, and the same red speckles lighted the ravine just enough so Lex could run without tripping over the bare roots of trees that twisted out of the high banks and lay across the path.

It was like being in a cellar, with the smell of earth around him. Or like being in a cave, he thought, a deep cave like the one in the Blue Mountains where Dad took me last year. The naked tree roots, hanging from the banks on each side, made him think of the queer icicles of stone that hung along the walls of Shenandoah caverns.

But the ravine was not a cavern, really. It was only a short, crooked gully. Before he could stop running, he was at the end of it.

The high banks flattened out. The trees were gone. The shelter of the darkness was gone, too. He was out once more in the red, awful daylight.

And the soldiers were between him and the river!

He could see them plainly. The bridge over the Potomac was burning at both ends. Other fires had sprung up since he left the attic window. Buildings that he didn't recognize were burning. And the British soldiers weren't in ranks; they were scattered everywhere; they carried blazing torches as they ran to kindle more fires.

He stood there without thinking about hiding—without even thinking that if he could see the soldiers, they could see him. Over and over, in his mind, one word repeated itself: Mother . . . Mother. . . .

For a while—for minutes, maybe, or perhaps for only a few seconds—Lex Landon wasn't an almost-grown-up man. He was just a fourteen-year-old boy, afraid, and lonely in his fear. He wanted to go home.

When Lex moved at last, he went straight toward the enemy. It seemed to him, all of a sudden, that the British soldiers didn't matter. All he thought was that they were between him and his mother, and he couldn't let them stop him.

He never knew exactly how he reached the river, nor how long it took him.

Later, he remembered, dimly, that there had been a

time when he was crawling through a swampy place where
saw grass slashed his face and fingers, and another time
when he was in a field where underbrush had been cut
down, and the sharp stubs, sticking up like nails in an
old board, gashed his feet. He'd crouched behind a brush
pile, then, to put his shoes on—and his shoes were gone!
He didn't know when he had lost them; but his shirt was
hanging open, and the three top buttons had been torn
off somehow.

He remembered hiding in a clump of burdocks in a
smelly barnyard, while a squad of soldiers hurried past
him, so close that he heard the rattle of their cartridge
boxes, their belts creaking, and their canteens bumping.

There had been other places where he'd hidden—
underneath a wagon—and then on his stomach in a ditch
beside a street all red and smoky with the flames of burning buildings.

Lex remembered the ditch best, because he'd stayed
there a long time, poking his head out like a turtle to look
up and down the street.

At last there'd been a moment when the street was
clear of soldiers, and he'd taken a deep breath and held it.
He didn't know why he had held his breath. And he
could not remember crossing that last street, but he was
across it. He was running toward the red shine of the
river, and he wasn't breathing. His chest felt as if it
would burst open, but somehow he couldn't let his breath
go.

The next thing he knew, the hollowed-out bank of the
river gave way underneath him. He was falling.

He fell with his face in the soft tide muck. His mouth
and nose were full of wet mud. He could hear the noises

he was making as he struggled—noises like a toadfish grunting, flopping—noises like big bubbles breaking. Finally, he was on his hands and knees, and he was blowing muddy bubbles. He was gulping hot air, and the taste of smoke was even stronger than the foul taste of the ooze he'd swallowed.

As he knelt there, the mud trembled. It seemed to Lex that the whole surface of the river had tipped slowly sideways and then tipped slowly back the other way. His ears rang, and his head felt squeezed, as if two enormous hands had hit him on both ears at the same time.

The stunning crash of an explosion rolled across the river. When Lex looked over his left shoulder, up across the overhanging bank of the Potomac, he saw that the broad sheet of fire above the burning ships had been ripped up the middle. The ammunition in the navy yard was blowing up!

The vivid flash of the explosion had shown him a double row of straggly black posts stretching out into the river. He knew where he was! He had fallen down the high bank within fifty yards of the long wharf where he had left the log canoe.

The tide was out. There was a wide strip of bare, sleek, slimy mud between him and the far end of the wharf. If he tried to walk, he would sink in almost to his knees at every step. It would take him a long time to cross the tide flat, and the soldiers could see him easily.

Lex lay down on his stomach in the mud and started crawling toward the water. He moved like a turtle, using knees and elbows as if they were flippers, and lifting his head just a little, now and then, to make sure he was going in the right direction.

Even when he reached the water, he kept right on crawling. His head went under. He held his breath until his fingers couldn't touch the bottom. Then he began to swim, dog-fashion, very quietly and slowly.

The two tall, slanting masts of the canoe rose over him. His hand touched the low, familiar gunwale, but he didn't try to pull himself aboard. Even now, at the last minute, with escape so near, the soldiers might still see him and begin to shoot, or else come running out along the wharf.

He let himself sink, and paddled underneath the log canoe. He came up on the other side, in the dark shadows of the wharf. But he couldn't stay there. He had to get away, quickly, while the tide was ebbing. When the tide turned, it might carry the canoe ashore, or even push it upstream toward the blazing bridge.

He didn't dare to clamber up the wharf and cast off the mooring lines. Instead, he hung by one elbow on the gunwale while he untied the ropes and let the ends slide overboard. He didn't like to lose those lines, but he'd just have to leave them dangling from the pilings. Maybe, when the British Army had left Washington, he could come back and get them.

A terrible thought struck him. Maybe the British wouldn't leave. Maybe, when a foreign army took the capital of an invaded country, it just stayed there—and you didn't have a country any more. Lex didn't know. But his father had said, time and again, that this war with England wasn't just an ordinary war. Major Landon said it was a second War of Independence, and, if the Americans were beaten, the United States might cease to be a nation; it might lose its freedom and be nothing but a group of British colonies again.

For a moment, Lex was fiercely glad that Washington was burning. Surely, if the enemy intended to take back the colonies that they had lost, the British Army wouldn't be destroying this new city and its handsome buildings.

He clung to the gunwale with one hand and pushed the log canoe from one slippery, scaly piling to another toward the end of the long wharf. When he felt the current tugging at the canoe, he dropped back to the stern and took hold of the rudder with both hands and started swimming with his legs—not kicking, but squeezing them together like the two blades of a pair of scissors.

The canoe moved slowly. He was only two or three yards from the wharf when another shuddering explosion let go. It was louder than the first one. The river trembled, and the sky itself was ripped across the middle. From horizon to horizon, a bluish-white flash changed the color of the night. It made the red glare of the burning town look pale.

For one dazzling moment, Lex could see a mass of black and ugly storm clouds hanging low above the city. The bright flash and the shocking sound of this new blast had not been made by the exploding powder houses in the navy yard. They were made by the sudden, savage lightning and the roar of a Potomac thunder-gust.

Then the wind struck. The flames at both ends of the bridge blew flat across the water. The bare masts of the log canoe leaned over steeply.

In no time at all, the river that had been so smooth was boiling with big whitecaps, and the heavy hull of the canoe was rolling crazily. The rudder bucked in Lex's hands. If he tried to hold on, it would tear itself loose.

He made a wild lunge for the starboard gunwale, touched it, gripped it. The canoe was rolling in the opposite direction. The gunwale, rising, pulled him up. He flopped over it headfirst and went sliding helplessly along the steep slant of a thwart. A wave, white and hissing, broke across the portside, and he felt the water go pouring over him with all the force of a swift-running creek, and then come pouring back again as the hull plunged and wallowed.

Bail! he thought. She'll sink unless I do. But it was no use, and he knew it. The waves were toppling in across the gunwale. They would fill her faster than he could scoop out the water. I've got to head her up into the wind.

He realized for the first time that he had escaped! It didn't matter, now, if the whole British Army saw him. The log canoe had drifted so far from the shore that musket balls would plop into the river long before they'd traveled half the distance.

Lex was still in danger, but it was a kind of danger he knew how to handle. He crawled forward through the sloshing water and hauled on the rope that hoisted the big jib. He didn't dare to raise it all the way; the screaming wind might burst it into rags. But when the sharp triangle of the sail was only a few feet up the foremast, the long bowsprit turned into the wind. The crazy rolling stopped.

Lex crawled back to the seat locker in the middle thwart and found the bailing scoop. Hour after hour, he fought the water. For a while, the blue-white lightning flashes showed him a gray circle of rain all around him. Then the thunder-gust died out almost as suddenly as it had come.

The rain had not put out the fires in Washington. They blazed up again as fiercely as before the storm. With the burning rainbow in the sky behind him, Lex clamped the tiller underneath his arm and steered for the Virginia shore he could not see. . . .

The first faint streak of dawn was in the east when the canoe slid into soft mud. Even in the dark, he had come almost straight to Alexandria. A low point, thick with willows, hid the town; but he was less than half a mile upriver. He put out the anchor, went floundering ashore, and stumbled up a weedy bank into the road that curved around the willows and became the street on which the Landons' brick house faced the river.

Lex saw his mother standing on the front stoop. She was not expecting him to come walking down the street. She was looking out across the river, and she didn't see him till he reached the gate.

"Lex!" she cried. And then, the way she did when she was good and angry, she said, *"Alexander . . . Hamilton . . . Landon!* Where have you been?"

Her mouth set itself into a straight line. She was really angry. Lex didn't blame her.

"Washington," he said.

She looked him up and down. His face was streaked with grime. His eyes were red and swollen. All the buttons were gone from his shirt, now, and the torn legs of his trousers hung in flaps that showed raw cuts across his knees. And neither the river nor the rain had washed the sticky foulness of the mud out of his clothes.

"What happened to your hand?"

He looked at his left hand. It was clean enough to see the angry scratches of the saw grass on it. They smarted, but he had got used to them. When he looked at his other hand, he saw that blood was dribbling down the fingers. It was welling out around the thin end of the splinter from the smashed-in door. The sliver was sunk deep into his palm. He tried to pull it out and couldn't, and the pulling sent a sharp pain shooting up his arm.

"Lex! Your feet . . . they're cut to pieces!"

"Yes," he said. Now that he thought about them, they were hurting badly.

"Oh, Lex!" His mother's mouth stopped being a straight line. It was soft and gentle. Her lips quivered. "Don't just stand there, Lex."

She came running down the steps, and her arms opened wide. She didn't even make him go around to the back door and take his dirty clothes off in the kitchen.

Chapter 4

LEX GETS HIS WISH TO BE A SOLDIER

WHEN Lex woke up, he was so clean that he didn't recognize himself.

He was in his own room, and the sun was shining through the crisscross curtains at the windows. The curtains and the linen bed sheets were as white as snowdrifts.

His right hand was bundled up in a clean bandage. He wriggled his fingers, and felt the sore place where the splinter had been pulled out while he was asleep.

His legs were stiff; and his feet felt tight, as if he'd gone to bed with his shoes on. He flipped back the sheet. His knees and his feet, too, were done up in white bandages.

"Mother!" The excited cry came from the hall outside. That sister of his! She'd been peeking through the keyhole at him. "Mother, he's awake!"

"Hey!" he shouted. "Come on in, you monkey!"

Robin didn't really look like a monkey. She just acted like one, sometimes, climbing trees or swarming up the rigging of the Landons' schooner. Now she came bursting in and bounced up onto the edge of the high bed. Before she said a word, Lex knew that she was bursting inside, too. When she was excited, her blue eyes seemed to get as big as pansies.

"Lex! They're coming!"

"You don't have to yell," he told her, "and don't sputter, either." Robin's small tongue often ran so fast it stumbled. "Well, who's coming?"

"The British! They'll be here 'most any minute!"

"Stupid!" Lex didn't mean it, but he had to keep this snub-nosed little sister in her place. "They burned the bridge. They can't come."

"Stupid yourself! They're not using any old bridge. They're coming up the river! Warships! A whole fleet of warships. Aren't they, Mother?"

Lex saw his mother in the doorway. She was carrying the big black and gold tray that had been brought from China and was never used except for company. The tray was filled with dishes.

"Are they, Mother?" he asked. "Are the British coming?"

"Yes, son." Mrs. Landon set the tray down on the bed beside him. "Nobody knows how far they'll come, but they're working up the river. I don't know how many ships. Some folks say twenty; some say half a dozen. But two of the ships are big ones—frigates."

"They can't get this far," Lex said. "They can't come any higher up the river than Mount Vernon. Fort Washington will stop them."

Fort Washington was on the shore of the Potomac, just across from the white-pillared house where President Washington had lived.

"They burned President Madison's house last night," he said, and thought how awful it would be if they burned George Washington's old home.

"It wasn't last night, son. You've slept around the clock —and five hours more. It's Friday, and it's almost half-past ten. Come, eat your breakfast." She smiled at him, but her face looked strained and anxious. "You went to sleep before we got you up the stairs. We had to carry you."

Lex started on the pile of golden corncakes. With his mouth full, he stopped chewing while he listened to the noises outside. Wagon wheels were grating on the stoned slope of the waterfront. Oxcart axles screeched. Wooden freight sleds squealed along the cobbles. Whips were cracking, and Negro dockhands were chanting. There was more noise than he'd heard in Alexandria since the enemy closed up the Chesapeake. The only ships that came to the Potomac nowadays were privateers or the fast clipper schooners that had run the blockade, or the pinks and shallops that crept in and out along the rivers, playing a deadly game of hide-and-seek with British guard boats.

"What's that racket, Mother?"

"The merchants are unloading all their ships, Lex. They're sending all the goods in the warehouses into the back country just as fast as they can load the wagons."

"You mean everybody's leaving?"

"No, not everybody. A good many, though—the people who have carriages and horses. All day yesterday and last night, gigs and chariots and chaises were going out of town with everything that could be packed into them."

"On top, too," Robin broke in. "The Elliotts had all their feather beds tied on top of their coach. They even had iron cook pots hanging on the axles. And the Wallings had that big grandfather clock of theirs stuck halfway out the window." Robin's tongue was tripping over itself now. "But the ar . . . ar . . . army isn't g . . . g . . . going."

"Army!" Lex's fork stopped halfway to his mouth. "Is the army here? Is Dad here?"

"No," his mother answered. "People say the army's gone north, up toward Baltimore. Robin's talking about sailors. They came through town this morning—sailors and marines from our new frigate *Guerrière* in Philadelphia and the *Java* that's not finished yet in Baltimore."

"How many?" Lex asked. He was thinking of the scarlet column that had filled the street in Washington.

"Only a few hundred," Mrs. Landon said, "but they had some cannon." Her voice sounded brave and hopeful. "And they've got the very best of all our officers— Oliver Hazard Perry, David Porter and John Rodgers."

The names were familiar. They were names of heroes. Commodore Perry'd whipped the British on Lake Erie. Commodore Porter, in the old frigate *Essex*, had almost wiped out the British merchant fleet in the Pacific. And Commodore Rodgers was the highest officer in the whole United States Navy.

"The trouble is," Lex's mother went on, "that it's too late for them to stop the British ships. They're going to try to trap them in the river when they go back."

"But there's the militia!" Robin cried. "You didn't tell him about them. They're going to fight!"

"Militia?" Lex repeated. "The militia's gone."

"We've got some more militia." His mother's mouth was set in a tight line. "They call it a regiment. A *regiment!*" She sounded angry. Scared, too. "It's the exempts. It's a hundred boys too young to be in the real militia and gray-headed men and cripples. Children! That's what they are . . . just children and grandfathers! What can they do?"

"I guess I'm in that regiment," Lex said.

"Yes. Captain Cutcheon sent word for you to turn out for drill at noon. I told him that you couldn't."

"But I can. I've got to."

"No! No, Lex. With your feet all cut . . . your hand . . ."

"They don't hurt. Honestly, they don't. I've got to go. You know that, Mother."

He went.

He took his father's hunting rifle, with the long, eight-sided barrel, and he wore his father's faded old campaign coat that had been at Yorktown. The coat was as much too big for him as the long rifle was, but his mother pinned it up in places where the belt would hide the creases, and she moved the buttons over.

When Lex tramped out to the field where British soldiers had drilled long ago—before they marched across the mountains and were massacred with Braddock—he was almost the only one of the "exempts" that had a uniform of any kind. Most of them were schoolboys or old men; and the boys were either making brags and yelling and skylarking, or just standing around, silent and white-faced and frightened.

They carried their guns every which way. It looked to Lex as if there weren't two guns of the same kind in the

whole little regiment. Some were old French muskets
from the Revolution. Some were ancient Indian-trade
firelocks. Most of them were only rabbit guns and bird
guns. A lot of them were rusty, and a lot more didn't
have their flints or ramrods.

Lex knew this scrubby "regiment" was useless. If the
warships came, Alexandria would be completely helpless.
He made up his mind that Robin and his mother mustn't
stay here. But when he got home and said so, Mrs.
Landon just looked at him for a moment. Then:

"No, Lex. I'm a soldier's daughter. I'm a soldier's wife,
too. And I guess now I'm a soldier's mother. I'm not
going to run."

"You've got to, sometimes. That's what the Americans
did mostly, in the Revolution. They even ran at Trenton.
Dad did, too. He sneaked off in the middle of the night."

"Who told you that?"

"Joe Piery."

"And just *who* may he be?"

"He's an old man. He was in Washington. He was in
Captain Hamilton's battery at Trenton. He and Dad
were on the same gun."

"Stuff and nonsense! He was bragging, the way all old
men do."

"He wasn't! He was brave! He was the bravest man I've
ever seen."

"But he wasn't in the army."

"They wouldn't let him join the army. Just the same,
he fought the British. And he was the only one that fought
them."

"How do you know?"

"I was with him." Lex didn't see the startled, frightened look that came into his mother's face. "I was on the
same gun with him—just like Dad at Trenton." Lex was
bragging now, himself. "There was this old brass cannon
that the army left behind. I helped Joe Piery get it on its
wheels and point it down the street. We were going to
fight the British—only they came too quick for us. He
told me to run, but *he* stayed. He was over ninety years
old, but he took my musket and he stayed. He shot the
general's horse. I was there. I saw it."

"Lex Landon, I could thrash you! You'd no business
being there!"

"I'm in the army now."

"Army! Little boys and old men! I told Captain
Cutcheon it's just murder. What are you shaking your
head about, Lex Landon?"

"I don't think anybody's going to get killed," Lex said.
"We'll run. We'll have to run."

"Well, then. What's the use . . . ?"

"Only I can't run," Lex said. "I can't unless you and
Robin are already gone."

"I declare, Lex! You're just like your father. No
matter what I say, you've got an answer for it."

"Yes, ma'am. Will you go, then?"

"We'll see," his mother said. Lex turned away. "Now
what are you up to?"

"We've got fifteen casks of prime tobacco in the *Lex
and Robin.* I'm going to unload them. I'm going to find
our dockhands and clean out the warehouse, too." He
stood in the doorway, thinking. "We've got three wagons.
If I load one of them light, and put the best team on it,

we can have it back here before noon tomorrow. One of those big freighter wagons will hold all the furniture in this house, Mother. It will, won't it?"

"Yes. Yes, I suppose so." Then her hands clenched, and she pounded them together. "Lex . . ."

"What?" He'd never realized how small her hands were, till she made fists of them. For the first time in his life, Lex felt stronger than his mother. He felt older, wiser. It was his job to protect her.

"I don't want to run," she said. "It doesn't seem right, with your father fighting."

"He ran. Lots of times. He had to."

"We'll see," his mother said again.

"Well, anyway," Lex said, "you can start packing, can't you?"

"Yes." She was unwilling, but her mouth was smiling. "When your father's home again, I don't know what on earth I'm going to do. I don't know what I'm going to do, with *two* big men around to argue with me."

"No, ma'am." Lex was grinning. "I don't either."

Far into the night, he worked in the hold of the *Lex and Robin,* hoisting out the precious cargo of tobacco, and then in the choking heat of the big Landon warehouse.

When the last loaded wagon rolled away, he tumbled into bed and slept for two hours. Then the squawking of a trumpet woke him. Somewhere, Captain Cutcheon had found a battered Revolutionary bugle and was using it to rouse out the new regiment of home guards. He had found a drum, too.

The old man who beat the drum was so stiff-jointed that he couldn't march. While the hundred boys and grayheads drilled that morning, the drummer sat in a rocking chair beside the drill field and beat out the orders. But it seemed to Lex that the deep, stirring thunder of the drum was just about the only military thing there was about the awkward, stumbling little crowd.

Soon after noon, the first of the Landon wagons came back empty, and Lex helped to load it with the chairs and tables, boxes full of dishes and his sister's dolls, rugs and whale-oil lamps, trunks and bundles, and even rakes and shovels. Only the beds were left.

Lex felt better as the wagon jolted off toward Fredericksburg. He told himself that he had done a man's job. But he had lost an argument. His mother wouldn't listen to him when he said that she and Robin should go with the wagon.

"There's no use talking," she said. "I'm not going. And that's that."

The trumpet squawked again in the late afternoon. The old drum rumbled. Captain Cutcheon shouted himself hoarse. The militiamen were going through the twenty-nine drill motions that a soldier had to know in order to load and fire his musket, when they heard a sound that wasn't like the deep growl of the drum. It was more like the slamming of a heavy door, a long way off.

They stood still, listening. The drummer laid his padded sticks on his fat stomach. The captain cupped a hand around his ear.

The distant slamming came again. It wasn't one door, now. It was three, almost together.

Lex heard somebody say, "Cannon."

"Attention!" Captain Cutcheon shouted. "Those

aren't cannon. Those are mortars! They're sea mortars on the British warships, and they're bigger 'n any cannon. They throw shells that weigh two hundred pounds—shells thirteen inches thick that go almost a mile up in the sky. When they fall and burst, those shells don't leave a smidgen of the biggest brick house any of you've seen."

A kind of shiver ran along the ranks. A scared boy dropped his gun. Captain Cutcheon cleared his throat.

"Maybe I oughtn't to be telling you all this," he said, "but you might's well know what's going on. The Britishers are using mortars on Fort Washington, that's what. Maybe the fort can fight 'em off. Maybe it can't. But if they come this far upriver with those mortars, they can blow this town of ours to kingdom come in fifteen minutes. And there's nothing we can do about it—not a hundred of us." The white-haired captain's voice broke. He put one hand up to his wrinkled face and wiped away the tears. "You might's well go home, boys."

The crooked lines began to break up, but nobody'd taken more than three steps when the drill field shook. Under Lex's feet, the hard earth shuddered. All around him, men and boys were staring southward toward the fort they couldn't see. A thick black smudge was rising slowly into the clean sky.

An hour later, a man who had been down the Potomac as a lookout galloped into Alexandria on a horse so thickly covered with sweat lather that it looked as if it had been smeared with harness soap. He pulled up in Market Square.

"They blew up Fort Washington!" he shouted. "Not

the British—our men!" His voice was shrill with anger. "Not one shell had touched 'em, but they blew the fort up! They didn't fire a single shot—just blew it up and ran. The cowards . . . cowards . . . *cowards!* There ain't nothing now to keep the Britishers from wiping out this town."

Chapter 5

LEX TRIES TO SINK A SHIP TO SAVE IT

Twenty ships were sinking.

For a mile along the river, they were going down—brigs and shallops, sloops and pinks, Hampton flats, and the proud Chesapeake Bay clippers.

On this Sunday morning, Alexandria was scuttling its own ships to keep the enemy from getting them.

The men who owned them and had sailed them stood in silent groups along the wharves and watched. Nobody felt like talking. It was hard to realize that these familiar ships were going to the bottom. Minute by slow minute, they were settling lower in the water.

Even the tall clippers and the brigs began to look like shallow scows, and then like rafts. Finally the sparkling current flowed across their decks.

46

Lex Landon saw it all from the front window of his room. He wanted to be down there on the waterfront, where the excitement was, but he felt ashamed to go. It didn't seem right for the Landon schooner to be lying at her wharf while other people's boats were being sunk. But his mother wouldn't let him sink the *Lex and Robin*.

"We're not going to scuttle our ship," she said firmly. "It's all wrong. Sinking all those boats just shows the British that we're scared to death of them. It's like . . . it's like blowing up Fort Washington. It's like quitting."

"It isn't quitting," Lex said. "It's one way of fighting. If they're sunk, they can't be captured."

"Fiddlesticks! If you sink the *Lex and Robin*, what will you do with her when the British go away?"

"I'll raise her."

"There!" his mother cried. "You see? That's exactly what will happen. If the British want those sunken ships, they'll raise them."

Lex could not believe it. He knew it would take days of hard work to pump out a sunken ship and float her. But his mother's mind was made up, and he couldn't change it. He didn't change his own mind, either.

It was Sunday evening when the British Fleet came up to Alexandria—six ships in column, their sails like white clouds and their brasswork gleaming in the sunset.

Two of them were frigates—big, square-rigged three-masters. Their gun ports were open. The red-painted muzzles of their cannon were pushed out.

The next ship was a smaller cruiser. With her two masts and her square sails, she looked like any ordinary brig. Lex, standing on the riverbank, saw something strange about her. Underneath her open gun ports, there was another row of smaller, square holes all along her side.

The three other ships were even stranger. They were low and ugly, and the stern half of each one was twice as high above the water as the front half. Their hulls looked like a backwoods farmer's clumsy, homemade shoes.

When the fleet dropped anchor, the two frigates and the brig lay with their bows upstream. Their long rows of cannon pointed straight at the defenseless town. Lex began to count them . . . eighteen guns along the side of the first frigate, nineteen on the second, and nine on the brig.

"How many?" Lex turned and saw Captain Cutcheon at his elbow. The captain wasn't wearing his blue uniform; he was dressed in a linen coatee and tobacco-colored trousers. "My eyes aren't so good," he said. "How many broadside guns, young Landon?"

"Forty-six," Lex answered.

"That's forty-six more than they need," the captain said. "Keep your eye on those bombs, Landon."

"Bombs?"

"Those three mortar ships. That's what they call 'em—bombs."

The three queer, stubby ships were turning so their bowsprits pointed at the town.

"That's how they aim the mortars," Captain Cutcheon said. "They aim the whole ship at the thing they want to hit."

Over the low bulwarks, Lex could see two huge iron mortars on the foredeck of each vessel. They looked as big as barrels . . . bigger . . . bigger even than tobacco hogsheads. They must be twenty times as big as the brass cannon in the street in Washington. They squatted on their haunches like black-metal elephants, with their flat noses pointed toward the sky.

Out at the end of the town wharf, a man began to wave a white flag on a pole.

"I've got to go now," Captain Cutcheon said. "The Mayor's going to surrender Alexandria. He wants me along. I kind of wish he didn't. I was in the army eight years, in the Revolution. We got licked right often, but this will be the first time I've surrendered."

Lex watched him and three other men get into a flat-bottomed skiff and row out to the frigate at the head of the long line of anchored warships. While they were gone, a few young boys turned war into a great adventure of their own. In their underwear, they swam out to the fleet and paddled all around it, whooping and hollering and waving their hands at sailors on the decks above them. Some of the sailors waved back. It wasn't like a war; it was more like a picnic.

When the boys swam ashore, they knew the names of all the ships. The frigates were *Seahorse* and *Euryalus*, and the brig was *Erebus*. The three mortar vessels had names that matched the dreadful things that Captain Cutcheon said about them—*Aetna, Meteor,* and *Devastation.*

The names also matched the news that Captain Cutcheon and the Mayor brought back from the flagship. Alexandria was being held for ransom, like a child who had been kidnaped or like people who'd been taken prisoner by pirates. If the ransom wasn't paid, the town would be destroyed.

The price was high. The enemy demanded 16,000

pounds of flour, 150 bales of cotton, and 1,000 hogsheads of tobacco. All the property that had been taken out of town must be brought back and given to the British.

Mrs. Landon had been right about the scuttled ships. The British were not going to raise them; they had an even better idea. They said that the Americans themselves must do it. They would burn Alexandria, they said, unless the people of the town refloated all the ships, repaired the damage, and then loaded them with all the plunder taken by the enemy.

"You see now, don't you, Lex?" his mother asked. "That's why I said it wasn't any use to sink them."

"Yes, ma'am," Lex said. "I see." But what he saw was something different. What he saw was that the enemy would take the *Lex and Robin* first of all.

They'll not! he told himself. They're not going to get her! Anyway, not first!

Lex went to bed, but he did not sleep. When the house was quiet, he got up and dressed, and tiptoed quietly downstairs and out the door.

Lights on the British warships made a row of yellow spatters in the river. But nobody saw him as he crept aboard the Landon schooner.

The dark didn't bother him. He knew every passage-way and ladder in the *Lex and Robin*. He was glad, now, that he had forgotten to take out the carpenter's chest when he was unloading the tobacco. There was a big auger in it, half as tall as he was.

He crawled backward through the hatchway into the low space between the cargo deck and the curved bottom of the schooner. The sharp point of the auger bit into a plank.

The timbers of the schooner had been cut from old, white iron oaks, and the trees had got their name because they were almost as hard as pig iron. It took Lex a long time to bore through the tough wood.

He was panting when the auger finally gouged down into the river. A cool jet of water spurted up. It felt good on his hot face and his burning hands.

One hole, though, wouldn't be enough to sink the *Lex and Robin* before daylight. He wished he knew how many it would take. Twenty, probably. Maybe more. Would he have time for twenty? He had left the house a little before midnight. By five o'clock, there would be light enough for lookouts on the British ships to see the schooner sinking. Five hours. If each hole took fifteen minutes . . . Twenty holes!

"Grits and gravy!" he said. The words boomed in the shallow, cramped space. They sounded big and brave. "I'm going to do it! They're not going to get her! Not first!"

The spurting water gurgled in the dark. It sloshed along the planks and soaked his knees. But it was just a thin stream, and it deepened very slowly. Hurry!

His hands were already smarting. Every now and then he dabbed them in the water, and the coolness eased the pain a little. But he felt the blisters swelling.

Lex was working on the seventeenth hole when he heard faint thumping noises overhead. He sat back on his heels to listen.

He was shoulder-deep in water. The *Lex and Robin* must have settled two feet. She was sinking faster, now, with water coming in through sixteen holes. In another hour . . .

But he didn't have another hour. He heard boots on the cargo deck an inch above his head. An iron lantern, speckled with a hundred small holes, dangled through the hatch. A pair of legs in short black gaiters and white breeches started down the ladder. A hard voice said:

"Nah, then. Come on out o' there, ye sneakin' Yankee." The freckled light fell on the barrel of a pistol. "Stir y'rself. Come along, nah, or we'll close the hatch an' leave ye here to drown."

Lex crawled toward the lantern on his knees.

"Up the ladder with ye! Quick!" The pistol jabbed him in the ribs. A hand came through the hatch and got him by the collar, twisted it, and hauled him up. A voice behind him said, "Quick march! Get topside, an' no tricks!"

The twisting fist shoved him toward the ladder to the upper deck. As he began to climb, the sharp point of a bayonet went through the bottom of his breeches. Lex yelped, but he scrambled faster. He came up into dim gray daylight and a ring of men in red coats and white crossbelts.

They were different from the British soldiers he had seen in Washington. They wore high, cone-shaped hats that looked almost like dunce caps, excepting that they didn't quite go up into a point, but ended in a flat, round top.

Lex didn't know that these men were marines. He only knew that they had caught him, and that he was in bad trouble.

"Back to the ship," a man with sergeant's chevrons on his sleeves said. "We'll have a hanging before breakfast, likely. That'll teach this Yankee town a lesson."

They took Lex by both arms and hustled him across the deck. The schooner was so low in the water that they stepped right from the deck into a boat alongside.

The boat rowed toward the brig. As the *Erebus* loomed closer, Lex tried to keep from thinking about what might happen to him. He tried to think instead about the row of small, square openings below the gun ports where the muzzles of her cannon pointed at the town. He'd never seen a ship with holes like that along her side. They were the same shape as gun ports. They weren't big enough for cannon, though, and all of them seemed empty.

The small boat slid smoothly alongside the brig. A rope ladder dangled. The sergeant grasped it and began to climb.

"Up with ye!" The pistol prodded Lex again.

As he clambered up the ladder, one of those mysterious openings was only a few inches from his head. Inside, he saw the gleam of metal—the shiny round end of a tube that slanted down into the ship.

Lex had time for only one quick glimpse. Then he was standing on the deck of the *Erebus*. His soaked clothes were dripping on the scoured white planking, and his shoes were oozing water. The sergeant was talking to a blue-coated officer.

"The schooner's done for, sir. There's near three feet of water in her. Here's the one that did it."

"Just a boy," the officer said. "Did he put up a fight?"

"No, sir. He came along as gentle as a lamb."

"How old are you?"

"Fourteen," Lex said. He didn't mention the three months going onto fifteen. Maybe, if they thought that he was just a boy, they wouldn't hang him.

"What's your name?"

Lex opened his mouth to answer. Then he closed it. He remembered that the British had been burning the homes of American militia officers. If he told his name, they'd find out that his father was a major in the army.

"I see." The officer looked hard at Lex. In his solid, brick-red face, the man's eyes were small and bright and hard. "You live in Alexandria, I suppose, and you're afraid somebody will be punished for what you have done. That's very likely. There are heavy punishments for doing what you did—destroying the King's property."

"It's not King's property!" Lex said.

"Ah, but it is. The town surrendered. Everything in it is King's property. And if the King's property is damaged, the town will be burned." Lex felt as if the hard, bright eyes were biting into him like augers. "When you sank that schooner, you broke the terms of the surrender. Did you know that?"

"No, sir."

"You know it now. And you'll have time to think about it. If the town's burned, you can blame yourself. Sergeant . . ."

"Yes, sir."

"Lock him up."

With the sergeant ahead and a marine behind him, Lex climbed down ladder after ladder. Heat and smells rose up to meet him. Deep inside the ship, the air was like an oven.

Lex was already sick with worry over what he'd done. The foul smells made him sicker, but he still had wits enough to know that *Erebus* was different from any other ship he'd ever seen. On both sides of the dimly lighted lower deck, long rows of wooden boxes slanted upward through the deck above. They looked a good deal like the box traps that boys made for catching rabbits, only ten times bigger. And their bottom ends were made of iron, with flat lids on them like the iron doors of an oven. But Lex could not imagine what they were.

There was another hatchway and another ladder going down—down into blackness. Heavy hinges grated. A hand between his shoulder blades pushed Lex into a cell no bigger than the smallest closet. The door closed behind him, and a bar clanked.

Lex was in the smothering black cell four days and nights. It was the worst time he had known in all his life. It was even worse than the hours in the hot darkness of the attic, in the empty house in Washington, when he had thought the house was burning.

In the attic, he'd been able to hear sounds. He'd been able to look through the little window at the burning city. But now he couldn't see even the hands which sometimes pushed a pan of food through a slit in the barred door. Except for the footsteps of the unseen man who brought the food, the only sound he heard was the faint swashing of the river on the ship's side when the tide was ebbing.

Lex lost track of time. In the dark, the days and nights got all mixed up. He thought that he'd been in the cell for seven days.

Had the town been burned because of what he did? Had the British found out who he was and burned his home?

All Lex knew, for certain, was that *Erebus* at last was moving. He could feel the stir and the straining of her timbers.

It was almost noon following his four days imprisonment when he was hustled up on deck. After being in the solid darkness for a hundred hours, he was as blind as any bat. The bright sun hurt his eyes. The dazzle of light on the water made the tears come.

Then, blinking and squinting, he saw that *Erebus* was sailing down the river, and one of the mortar ships was with her. Already, they were miles from Alexandria; and Lex heard the sound of guns.

A headland pushed out from the Virginia shore. As *Erebus* came round the point, Lex saw a cloud of smoke above a bank of raw, red dirt. Another cloud hung over four ships in the river. Flashes darted toward each other from the two clouds. Thunder rolled across the water.

The *Erebus* was moving steadily down the Potomac. The red bank of earth came nearer. It was not a fort. It wasn't even a complete wall. It was only piles of dirt, with hollows in between them, but Lex saw the snouts of cannon in the hollow places. Every now and then, a yellow flash winked, and a spurt of smoke jumped toward the British warships.

Suddenly, as Lex watched, one of the big heaps of earth exploded. He could see it fly to pieces. Where it had been, the barrel of a cannon stuck up like a leaning tree trunk.

"Hah! They caught it that time!"

Lex looked around.

"How'd you like that, Yankee?" The marine who guarded him was grinning. "How'd you like to be up on that hill now?"

"I'd like it," Lex said. Right now, he'd like nothing better than to point a cannon at these people who had kept him in that stinking-hot cell. But he was surprised that any Britisher could act so friendly. For the first time, Lex noticed that this fellow in the red coat and white crossbelts wasn't much more than a boy. He had a round face and a mouth so small it made Lex think of Robin's. And even in his high, peaked hat, he wasn't as tall as the bayonet fixed on his shiny musket.

"I bet you'd like it," the marine jeered. "That there was a mortar shell. A big un. An' there goes another."

A gush of smoke leaped upward from the low forward deck of one of those strange-looking ships. The shell it fired climbed up into the sky. Lex could see it plainly— a big, round, black ball with brown smoke like a tail behind it. Far up in the clear sky, it seemed to stop. It seemed to hang there. Then it turned. It began to fall, slowly at first, and then swiftly and more swiftly. Just above the piles of dirt, it burst. The sound it made was more than an explosion—it was a terrible, wild scream as the broken pieces of the iron shell went flying through the air. To Lex, hearing it for the first time, it sounded as if many men had been hurt and were crying out in pain.

"You ain't seen nothin'," the marine said, "till you've seen the *Erebus* cut loose with her rockets."

"Rockets?"

"That's what I said, Yankee. There ain't no ship in the whole world like this un. Those mortar ships ain't nothin', alongside of *Erebus*. She shoots lightnin', that's what. She shoots sheets of fire . . . whoosh! Where the fire hits, there ain't nothin'. Ships, towns, anythin'—they're gone. Like that . . . whuff!"

"Did you . . . ?" Lex choked on the question. He was afraid to hear the answer. "Did you burn the town?"

"Me?" The marine grinned again. "Not me. I didn't have no matches." Then the grin was gone. "You live in that town where we was?"

"Yes."

"You been worried, huh? I dunno if I should tell you, but we didn't burn it. All we burned was one ship."

"Thanks," Lex said. He felt weak with relief. "Which ship did you burn?"

"I dunno. A brig, she was. They couldn't raise her. But we fetched off all the others." The English boy looked all around to make sure nobody could hear him. "Don't you go blabbin' about this. You hear? We didn't fetch away the schooner that you sank. Her moorin' lines were still tied to the wharf when she went down. They flipped her over on her side. Too much work to raise her, capsized like she was. An' there wasn't nothin' left to burn—only the tops of her masts stickin' out, an' a few feet of rail."

Lex almost yelled with joy. Just in time, he remembered that he mustn't act as if his guard had told him anything.

"Thanks," he said in a low voice. "Thanks!"

"Well, anyhow, you've still got a home, an' a boat, too—if you ever get back to 'em. In about five minutes, now, those Yankee cannon will be shootin' at us. How you goin' to like that—bein' shot at by your own guns?"

"I'll like it," Lex said stoutly. "I'll like it if they hit us."

"Not much you will. You ain't been shot at, or you wouldn't say that. It ain't fun, bein' shot at . . . splinters flyin' . . . an' men gettin' mashed. You never know when it'll be your turn." Suddenly the round face tried to look stern. "Shut up, Yankee!"

A rush of sailors came along the deck. An officer was shouting orders. Men went scrambling up the rigging. The sails of the rocket ship began to vanish, furled up tight against the spars.

Lex heard the anchor cable rumbling out. The *Erebus* swung quickly in the current. Her bows pointed up the river. Over her high larboard bulwark, Lex could see the heaps of red earth plainly. He could see men like a swarm of ants behind them. Those must be the seamen from the new United States ships up at Baltimore and Philadelphia. They were swinging shovels. They were cutting down trees. They were dragging hewn logs into the unfinished earthworks. The Americans weren't licked yet! They weren't going to let the British ships get out of the Potomac.

Whoo-o-ooshhh! The sudden, rushing sound was like the first blast of a thunder-gust. It seemed to Lex that the whole side of the *Erebus* had burst into flame. A sheet of fire leaned out across the river. For a moment, it shut out the wooded shore, the heaps of red earth and the guns between them, and the swarm of sailors.

Then the slanting sheet of fire was gone. Against the blue sky, twenty trails of dark smoke curved toward the American entrenchments. Flashes leaped up all along the dirt piles. In the field behind them, the dry grass took fire. The underbrush in front of them began to burn in half a dozen places. But the rockets hadn't driven the Americans away. The shovels were still swinging. He could see men running down the hillside, beating out the fires to keep the smoke from blinding the gun pointers.

He could see a gun crew heaving at the wooden carriage of a cannon. He could see the barrel of the cannon turning slowly till it aimed at the *Erebus.* Smoke spouted from its muzzle.

Lex heard a wailing cry. It sounded like a hurt dog howling a long distance off. He didn't know that he was hearing, for the first time, the sound that a solid-iron ball from a cannon made when it was coming toward you.

The howling stopped. A new noise took its place—a noise like a whole nest of hornets buzzing. A white blur whizzed across his face. There was something different about the bulwark of the ship. He could see the river through it! Lex stared at the jagged hole in the thick timbers. Then he yelled:

"Yi-iahh! They hit us!" Who said Americans could not fight? Who said they always ran away? "Yi-iahh! Yi-i-iaa-ahhh! They hit us!" He turned fiercely to the young marine beside him. "And I like it!"

The English boy's red face had turned as white as paper. His soft mouth was open, and a little blood was dribbling on his chin. There was more blood on his neck and on his collar, and a thin bright stream was running down his face. The end of a long splinter stuck out from his cheek. He said "O-oww" in a small, surprised voice. Through his open mouth, Lex saw the other end of the thin splinter pressed down on his tongue. The boy mumbled again:

"O-oww. Out. Pull . . . out."

"It'll hurt," Lex said.

The round face nodded. The boy's eyes were as blue as Robin's. It's queer, Lex thought. We're enemies. But he's expecting me to help him. The blue eyes trusted him just as his sister's did.

Lex put one hand on the marine's cheek and pressed hard. With the other hand, he gave the splinter a quick, steady pull. It came out, and the blood ran faster.

"Thank you. You're a bit of all right, Yankee."

"I'm not a Yankee," Lex said. "I'm a Virginian. It's only people in New England that are . . ."

Whoo-oo-ooshhh! The sound that was like a hurricane blast blew Lex's voice away. Twenty more of those fire-spitting rockets curved across the river. As they burst, the flash and crackle of explosions ran along the streak of raw earth.

All afternoon, the mortar shells climbed up into the sky. All afternoon, the *Erebus* hurled out her flights of rockets. Her cannon joined the thunder of the other ships' guns.

But the Americans fought on. When the sun went down, the British Fleet was still trapped in the river.

Chapter 6

ON THE FLAGSHIP OF THE ENEMY

Prisoner to the quarterdeck!"

The midshipman who had brought the order jabbed Lex with his knuckles.

"Get along, you! On the double!" The knuckles jabbed again. The blows didn't hurt. They only made Lex angry. The fist that hit him wasn't any harder than his tomboy sister's. It was not much bigger, either. The midshipman looked as if he should be playing games in somebody's backyard, instead of giving orders on a warship. "You'll learn not to cheer when British ships get hit. Captain Bartholomew is going to skin you. Ever had a flogging, Yankee?"

On the quarterdeck, Lex faced the officer who'd told him Alexandria might be destroyed because he'd damaged the King's property.

"I saw what you did this afternoon." The captain's

voice was stern. His next words took Lex completely by surprise. "You helped the sentry when he had been wounded. I'm a fair man, and I'm taking notice of it. I gave you four days punishment for doing something wrong. Have you thought it over?"

"Yes, sir." In those endless days and nights, Lex had done a lot of thinking. "What I did was not wrong. I didn't break the terms of the surrender."

"Indeed. How do you figure that out?"

"I know when Captain Cutcheon and the Mayor brought the terms back from the flagship. It was after dark. I don't believe the town accepted them that night."

"Hmm. Just the same, I could have hanged you. The town had been captured, and the ships were prizes. And you're not a soldier, so you had no right to fight us."

"I did! I am a soldier. I'm in the militia."

"But you weren't in uniform when we took you."

"Most of the militia don't have uniforms."

"Well, Landon," Captain Bartholomew said, and then he smiled a little at the startled look on Lex's face. "Yes, I know your name. I know your father is a major in your army. Your mother wrote a letter. I told her that we couldn't turn you loose, but I assured her that we wouldn't hang you. Have you had enough of the cell, Landon?"

"I can stand it," Lex said stubbornly. He wasn't going to admit how terribly he dreaded that black hole.

"It hasn't changed your mind? You'd sink that schooner again, if you had the chance. Is that it?"

"Yes, sir."

"And you'd like to see this ship sunk, too, even if you're on her?"

"Yes, sir!"

"Good for you, young Landon. That's the way you ought to feel about it, when your country is at war. I don't want to lock you up again. Will you give me your word, as an officer's son, that you will not try to escape?"

"Not ever?" Lex asked. He knew that even before war began, some Americans had been kept on British ships for years.

"We'll make it seven days. Your word of honor until sunset, one week from today. By that time, we'll be in the Chesapeake again. I don't believe you can do much escaping in the bay."

"I'll give my word," Lex said. The bay was big, but it was not so wide he couldn't get away by swimming. When the week was over, he'd find some way to escape.

Lex slept on the bare deck that night. When he woke up in the morning and looked through a gun port, it was almost as if he had waked up in his room at home and looked out the window. All the ships from Alexandria were anchored in the river. They didn't look as if they had been sunk and raised again.

All of them were flying two flags, one above the other. The flag on top was British, with the Stars and Stripes below to show that the ships were captured.

It was a sight Lex Landon never would forget. His hands clenched into fists. His country's flag, shamed! When he tried to count the ships, his eyes blurred. Eighteen . . . nineteen . . . twenty . . . *twenty-one* ships with the Stars and Stripes in disgrace beneath a hostile banner!

And then down the river came the *Seahorse* and the *Euryalus*. Their white pyramids of sails towered over the *Erebus*. Big and beautiful and deadly, the two frigates steered toward the Americans' crude earthworks. The guns of both ships roared almost together.

And now *Erebus* was moving. Her sails flapped and filled. Her bows swung toward the shore. She was going in to help the mortar ships and frigates break the trap.

She went in close. Much closer than the *Seahorse* and the *Euryalus*. So close that Lex could see the faces of the cannoneers behind the piles of dirt. So close that when the whooshing sound burst from her side, the sheet of fire did not slant; it lay almost flat above the river.

The rockets didn't arch across the sky. They darted toward the shore like flaming arrows. But they were much bigger—thicker than a man's leg, longer than a musket. Lex could see some of them driving into the red dirt. They stuck there, smoking, spouting sparks, exploding. They looked like a crooked row of fence posts, burning.

The mortar ships were firing, too. The frigates' guns were pounding like enormous drums gone crazy. The cannon on the shore were answering the warships, but the British had more guns than the Americans. Four . . . five times as many.

More than forty cannon battering those heaps of loose dirt. And the mortars! Six of those enormous mortars, hurling shells that weighed two hundred pounds. And every few minutes, twenty of those flaming fence posts plunging down on the Americans.

The whole hillside seemed to be on fire. The smoke of the burning woods was mixed up with the smoke of bursting shells and rockets. Lex could see dirt flying like spray when the solid-iron shot smashed into the earthworks.

But the Americans were fighting just as if they didn't know the enemy was ten times stronger. They weren't even trying to protect themselves behind the piles of dirt. Some of them were dragging cannon closer to the river—three small field guns with brass barrels and high, narrow wheels.

The little cannon bounced across the rough ground. At the edge of the bare field, with nothing to protect them, the Americans wheeled the guns into a crooked line. Lex saw the three brass barrels turn until they pointed at *Erebus.*

Lex yelled then. He couldn't help it.

"Yi-iahh! Yi-iahh!" He didn't have a guard today. In the din of firing, nobody could hear him. There was nobody to stop him when he climbed the bulwark and went scrambling up the rigging. He clung to the ropes and watched the row of brass guns. "Come on! Give it to 'em!"

Three puffs of smoke bulged out. The little guns jumped and rolled backward. They must have made a noise—at least a small noise—but Lex didn't hear it in the thunder of the bigger cannon.

Instead, he heard a kind of flutter in the air. It sounded as if someone had said "Pfwaa-aahh" close to his ear. The ratlines to which he was clinging shook. Then, suddenly, they sagged. Lex almost lost his hold. A few inches from his face, he saw the broken ends of tarred ropes dangling. One of the solid-iron balls from the battery onshore had cut them just as neatly as if a sharp knife had sliced them.

It might have killed me, Lex thought. If I'd been a little higher, it would have gone right through me. He ought to be afraid. I *am* afraid, he thought. But not the way I was in Washington. Maybe it's because there isn't anyplace to hide, now. Maybe it's because I know that I can't run.

But that wasn't true. He *could* run. He could drop to the deck. He could run to the nearest hatchway. He could hide somewhere, deep down inside the ship. He could be safe there—safer, anyway—with the thick timbers of the *Erebus* between him and the howling cannon balls.

No! he thought. No! No, I can't! For one cold, sickish moment, Lex was afraid that he was going to run. The British seamen wouldn't notice him; they were much too busy. Nobody'll ever know it, if I run. But I'll know.

He began to climb again. As he pulled himself up past the shot-torn ropes, he felt the ratlines shudder. The whole ship shook as her guns went off. Their smoke came swirling up around him, choking, blinding. He began to cough. The bitter smoke made tears run down his cheeks.

Dimly, on the shore, he saw the first flash of a bursting shell above the crooked row of field guns. And then, faintly in the awful roar all up and down the line of British ships, he heard the whhrraa-annghh! of the explosion. It was like a great iron hammer falling on a huge iron kettle, and the kettle breaking, all the pieces clanging.

Flash . . . whhrraa-annghh! Flash . . . flash . . . the hot, yellowy-red flashes overlapping one another, and the rending, ripping sounds of the shells all mixed up together . . . whhrraa . . . whhrraang . . . whhurraa-annghh . . . gughh!

Lex hung on with one hand. He used his other hand to wipe his smarting eyes, and then he waved it at the little guns lost somewhere in the smoke of the explosions.

When the smoke thinned, he saw that there was no longer any reason to wave at the brave guns.

All three of them were gone.

Where they had been, there was a raw hole in the red earth of the field.

By the middle of the afternoon, the fight was over.

A flag with fifteen stars and fifteen stripes still waved above the battered earthworks, but the piles of earth were only half as high as they had been at the beginning of the battle. They were streaked with furrows where the British shot had plowed them. In some places, they had disappeared completely. The Americans' few cannon had been smashed, tipped over. Some of them had disappeared, too. They were buried under tons of dirt.

The rocket ship was badly hurt. The jagged ends of broken planks bulged inward from her bulwarks, and long splintered gouges ran across her deck.

Other British ships had been hurt, too, but not one of them had been knocked out. They had broken the trap set by the Americans. The squadron started down the river.

Two days later, the *Erebus* was anchored in the midst of the main British Fleet. It stretched out for miles in all directions over Chesapeake Bay. The hundreds of bare masts and the spars with tightly folded sails made Lex think of the leafless woods on low shores of the Potomac River, when the spring floods made the water rise far up the tree trunks. The masts looked like a forest growing in the gray-green water of the bay.

"Didn't know we had a fleet like this, huh?" The young

marine beside him jogged his arm. "You Yankees might's well quit."

Lex looked at him. One side of his round face was swelled up two times bigger than the other. A bandage hid the wound made by the splinter Lex had pulled out. The white strip of cloth went up over his head, underneath his hat, and was tied in a knot with two long ends below his chin. It made his hat too small.

He was a funny sight, but Lex Landon didn't feel like laughing. He had already counted sixty ships, and there were still more that he hadn't counted. What could his country do against a fleet like this?

"That there's the *Tonnant*." The marine's high, black hat teetered as he pointed at a huge ship half a mile away. "Eighty guns, she's got. That's where the adm'rals an' the gen'ral are when they ain't chasin' Yankees, burnin' towns, and such. Hey, look!"

A long string of brightly colored flags was climbing toward the *Tonnant*'s masthead.

"That's our signal!" The wounded boy grabbed for his hat and caught it just before it toppled off his head into the bay. "That top flag means the adm'ral's sendin' out a message."

"Cockburn?" Lex asked.

"Uh-uh. Cochrane—Sir Alexander Cochrane. He's higher 'n Cockburn. An' that next flag means the signal is for us. It's for the captain of the *Erebus*. See?" The peaked hat tilted toward the quarterdeck. The rocket ship was sending up a single flag. "That means we got the message. Somethin' is goin' to happen."

"What?"

"How would I know? I ain't no midshipman." For a

moment, the boy's face was sullen. He pouted the way
Robin did in school when she was asked a question that
she couldn't answer. Lex knew the marine was ashamed
because the question showed he wasn't quite as smart as
he was letting on to be. "Only off'cers and midshipmen
can read all them flags. You'll find out soon enough. Just
stay around here, Yankee. You ain't goin' nowhere."

Lex found out.

And he was going somewhere.

Less than five minutes after the string of signal flags
was hoisted, he was being hustled into a small boat, and
the boat was pulling toward the *Tonnant*.

The captain of the *Erebus* was sitting on the stern
thwart. He looked very solemn.

Lex began to feel uneasy. He was thinking about the
long column of British soldiers marching into Washington. He was remembering how Joe Piery had said that the
officer in the blue uniform, on horseback, might be
Admiral Cockburn. Now he was being taken to the ship
where Cockburn lived. Had the British found out, somehow, that he'd been with Piery just before the old man
shot the general's horse? Had they found out, somehow,
that the musket Piery used had been *his* gun?

They couldn't have found out! But if they had . . .

Captain Bartholomew had said they could have hanged
him just for sinking his own father's ship. And now the
general whose horse was shot was on that ship ahead!

The sailors in the boat stopped rowing. The bulging
black side of the *Tonnant* towered up higher than the
tallest house in Alexandria. It seemed to Lex that it shut
out the sky.

From an entry port far up, a rope ladder dangled.

Captain Bartholomew began to climb, and then Lex was climbing, too, with the captain's white silk stockings just above him.

A bosun's pipe chirped like a startled bird. An armed guard waited on the deck. A lieutenant with a bony, hooked nose like a bird's beak saluted Bartholomew.

"The admiral is waiting, sir," he said.

Two men seized Lex by both his arms.

"No need of that," Bartholomew said. "He's given his parole."

The hands let go. Lex followed the two officers along a deck that swarmed with soldiers. A marine on guard beside a door presented arms. The door swung open.

Lex was in a cabin larger than the parlor of the Landons' house. The bright sun, reflected from the water far below, came through a row of slanting windows. It danced on the polished barrels of two cannon in the cabin. It glittered on the polished buttons and the gilded epaulets of officers who sat at a long table.

All the officers were looking at him. There was something odd about them. For a moment, he couldn't understand why two of them looked out of place.

Suddenly he knew! They were Americans!

One of them was a thick-shouldered, chunky man in a colonel's uniform. The pale-blue collar of his coat was almost black with sweat. One sleeve was dark from mopping at his face. The whole coat looked as if he'd slept in it all night.

The other man was younger and much thinner. His coat fitted better; but it, too, was stained and rumpled, and the single epaulet he wore was tarnished. His eyes were bloodshot, and the pinched-in corners of his mouth gave him the look of a man who hadn't slept at all for many nights. He was very different from the smiling, elegantly dressed young gentleman who came to Alexandria, one day last spring, to ask Major Landon to be a witness in a court case. But Lex recognized him by his long, fair hair that curled almost as softly as a woman's.

He was a lawyer and he lived in Georgetown and his name was Frank . . . Frank . . . Lex remembered that was what his father called the young man. He remembered that somebody else had come into the warehouse office and had called him Francis.

For the first time since the British caught him in the flooded hold of the *Lex and Robin,* he was seeing somebody he knew. He was seeing somebody from home—somebody who might know what happened to his father. He was still trying to remember the young lawyer's last name when the American colonel spoke out in a rasping voice:

"Well, gentlemen, congratulations. Admiral Cochrane . . . Admiral Cockburn . . . General Ross. . . . Here is the army that defended Alexandria. You captured all of it—one fourteen-year-old boy. A gallant victory!"

Lex saw the rumpled colonel's chin jut out between the high, soiled points of his wet collar. He saw the colonel's arm rise, and his fist start down as if to pound the table. Then one blunt, thick finger aimed itself at the officer in the scarlet coat.

The last time Lex had seen that coat, the general who wore it had been toppling backward, leaping from the saddle of his wounded horse.

"I repeat, General Ross, a gallant victory indeed! An old, sick man dragged from his bed and treated like a criminal!" The finger swung to one of the blue uniforms. "Admiral Cochrane, I repeat: congratulations! You now see the kind of war that Admiral Cockburn has been fighting. War against civilians! War by burning helpless villages at midnight! War by stealing hams and silverware and . . . Yes, I mean you!"

Lex saw the finger stabbing at another face across the table. Then the finger folded slowly, and the colonel's hand became a hairy and sweat-beaded fist in front of Admiral Cockburn's open mouth.

The last time Lex had seen that mouth, it had been open wider than it was now. Cockburn had been yelling orders to the soldiers to hunt down Joe Piery. Had the soldiers caught him? Did the colonel mean Joe Piery when he spoke about an old, sick man?

The fist came down upon the table, but it made no sound at all. It touched the table quietly and lay there, clenched. To Lex, its quietness seemed louder than the crash he had expected.

He expected an explosion of loud anger from someone. A British general and two British admirals surely wouldn't let a colonel of a beaten army talk to them like that! But the colonel went on talking. His voice changed. It was so low that his quiet words were like his fist. They sounded louder than if he had bellowed. The British officers were listening, too. They were looking at him as if . . . Grits and gravy! They were looking at him just as if they liked him!

"War on women, Admiral Cockburn. You know how many homes you've burned while women pleaded with you, on their knees. War on old men, General Ross. Dr. Beanes is sixty-five years old. And now war on children, Admiral Cockburn—on this boy you kidnaped. Your officers have treated both of them like convicts. Why? What is their crime? Dr. Beanes rounded up some stragglers from your army, General—from your *retreating* army. Yes, I said *retreating*.

"You didn't dare to stay in Washington. You didn't dare to hold one foot of ground in the United States. You knew you'd be cut off and captured, like Burgoyne at Saratoga and Cornwallis down at Yorktown. You were running for your ships so fast that you could not control your men. Dr. Beanes defended himself and his home town against drunken looters! Young Alexander Landon here was protecting his father's property from thieves. And for that, he's locked up like a thief himself!"

"S-sir . . ." Lex heard his own voice quavering. "I . . . I wasn't locked up all the time."

"Indeed." Admiral Cochrane looked at him sternly. "How long were you locked up?"

"I don't rightly know. But it's been a week since I was let out."

"Why are you telling us this, Landon?"

Lex liked the way the admiral called him Landon. It made him feel grown-up.

"I . . . I . . ." He tried to speak up like a man, but his tongue was stiff and clumsy. After all, not many fourteen-year-old boys talked up to an admiral commanding more than sixty warships. "It . . . it seems like the right thing to do. I wasn't treated bad . . . badly, I mean. Except at first." He remembered the hot, black cell on the *Erebus*. "But Captain Bartholomew said he could have hanged me, and he didn't. It seems like it's only fair to say so."

Lex knew instantly that he'd said something silly. As if

they couldn't see for themselves that Captain Bartholomew hadn't hanged him! They were laughing at him. At
least Cockburn was. The general was chuckling, and a
smile twitched Admiral Cochrane's mouth. Only the
American colonel glared at him as if he had done something wrong.

"I'm glad you said that, Landon." For a moment, the
commander of the British Fleet did not look like a high
and mighty admiral. He looked like a gentleman who was
going out of his way to be kind. "War is an ugly business.
There is very little that is fair about it. I'm glad you
wanted to be fair. Your name is Alexander, isn't it?"

"Yes, sir."

"And your father's name is Thomas?"

"Yes, sir."

"Colonel Skinner. . . . Mr. Key. . . ." The admiral
nodded at the American artillery lieutenant. Lex suddenly remembered seeing his name signed to a letter on
his father's desk—F. S. Key. Some people called him
Francis Scott Key. The admiral went on: "There is something I would like to say to both of you, gentlemen, and
to young Landon here as well.

"I have heard it said that when the British troops
surrendered at Yorktown, their bands played 'The World
Turned Upside Down.' It's still upside down! We ought
not to be fighting each other. This war was forced on
England. England did not declare war; the United States
did. Oh, I know . . . I know your reasons. I think they
are wrong.

"We ought to have been on the same side—both of us
fighting Napoleon. We speak the same language. We even
use the same names. Mine is Alexander, and I have a son

named Thomas—the same as this boy and his father, only turned around. My son is with me. He is captain of *Surprise*, frigate. For a few days, Colonel Skinner, you will be his guest. I am transferring you and Landon and Mr. Key . . ."

"Guest!" Skinner snorted. "You mean his prisoner! We came under a flag of truce. Do you intend to violate it?"

"I intend to do my duty. You would do yours, Colonel. You know that the force under my command is going to attack Baltimore. If I released you, sir, it would be your duty to warn your militia. You might succeed in doing it. That schooner of yours has a very pretty turn of speed. I'm sorry, gentlemen, but the necessities of war compel me to detain you until Baltimore is taken."

"You'll never take it!" Colonel Skinner told him.

"Oh, I rather think we will. I regret the inconvenience to you, gentlemen. But it will not last long; four or five days at the most."

"I say you'll never take it!"

"I have one more regret, sir," Cochrane said. "I'm sorry you are not on active service, Colonel Skinner, instead of being commissary for exchange of prisoners. If all Americans liked fighting half as well as you do, this might be a much more interesting war. There aren't many Yankees who talk to us as you do. It's so unusual that we listen to you. But it's not your talking or the names you've called us that have done the business. It's the letters you brought from the wounded officers we left behind at Bladensburg, saying they've been treated decently. And young Landon settled it by being fair about the way he has been treated. As soon as we have taken

Baltimore, I will release both Landon and your precious Dr. Beanes."

"I repeat, sir, you can't take it! Baltimore's not Alexandria. It's not Washington, either. By this time, the militia . . ."

"The militia!" Cockburn sneered.

"Thirty thousand of them," Skinner said.

General Ross leaned forward, smiling.

"Did you say thirty thousand, Colonel?"

"I did," Skinner answered.

"Hmmmm-hmm." Ross yawned. "Since you're going to be with us for a few days," he said blandly, "I can tell you something. You live in Baltimore, I understand. Too bad it's such a nest of pirates—privateers, you call them. This time a week, they'll be cleaned out. But that's not all of it. I've picked your city, Colonel, as the winter quarters for my army. I'll take Baltimore no matter if it rains militia."

Chapter 7

DARK WATER, AND A DESPERATE CHANCE

ALL night, the British Fleet sailed up the Chesapeake.

All night, Lex Landon leaned against the larboard bulwark of the frigate *Surprise* and watched the glare of fires along the shore.

Every few minutes, a new gush of sparks and flames leaped up out of the darkness. Sometimes it was a burning haystack. Other times it was a heap of brushwood, or a pile of fence rails.

And then, up the bay, another red glow would begin to spread. The chain of alarm fires, always stretching farther northward, was warning Baltimore that the attack was coming.

Watching them made Lex feel better. The British couldn't take the city by surprise.

He said so, once, to Mr. Key, when the young lawyer-soldier stopped pacing back and forth between two carronades and slumped against the bulwark for a minute.

"Yes," Mr. Key said, "Baltimore will know they're coming. I suppose that's better than not knowing anything—but not much better."

"Not much?" The gloomy words took Lex completely by surprise.

"No, Lex. I'm afraid not."

"But our army will be ready for them!"

"Ready where? We were ready, too, at Washington, but we were ready in the wrong place. We didn't know which way the enemy was coming until it was too late. They whipped our army piece by piece. Half of our men didn't get a chance to fight; they didn't fire a shot. The same thing can happen this time. Those signal fires can't tell our army where the British troops will land."

"But we've got more men than they have! Can't we have men all around the city?"

"I don't know. I hope so."

"How big *is* the British Army?"

"Six or eight times bigger than the one your father helped to beat at Trenton," Mr. Key said. "Maybe ten or twelve times bigger. It's stronger than any of the armies we defeated in the Revolution, at Saratoga or at Yorktown. I've heard everything from seven thousand men to fifteen thousand."

"We've got thirty thousand!"

"Have we?" Key laughed. The sound was short and sharp. It wasn't happy. "Where'd you get that notion?"

"Colonel Skinner said . . ."

"Oh. Skinner. He was bluffing, Lex. He was fighting

in the only way he could. He was trying to make the British think we are much stronger than we really are. It's a way to gain time. He was trying to make General Ross cautious, so the British Army will move slowly."

"Then it isn't true?"

"It's true enough—on paper. There are thirty thousand men on the militia lists, but names on paper don't win battles. It takes time to get the men together. It takes time to put them where they ought to be. The more slowly Ross's army marches, the more time Smith will have to meet it at the right place."

"Smith?"

"Sam Smith. He's a major general." Lex heard that hopeless laugh again. "A general who never won a battle! He's a merchant, really. A rich businessman in Baltimore. A banker. A big politician, too. He's been in Congress a long time—twenty years. He isn't young; he's sixty-two years old. He was a colonel in the Revolution. Now he's in command at Baltimore. If we only knew . . ." Beside him, in the darkness, Lex heard Mr. Key's hand pounding on the hollow bulwark. It made quick, soft noises like the sound of a man's palm slapping his leg nervously. "If we only knew where Ross is going to land! If we could only . . . If! *If!* Even if we knew, there'd be no way of getting word to Smith."

"We will know, when the soldiers go ashore."

"By that time, it will be too late." Key turned away to pace the deck again.

Lex stayed where he was. Slowly, one by one, he brought his fingertips down on the top plank of the bulwark. He was counting the days that had gone by since he gave his word that he wouldn't try to get away. Captain

Bartholomew himself had said the promise was for seven days.

Lex used up the fingers and the thumb of one hand. He started on the other. Six . . . seven . . . *eight!* His parole was over! It had ended hours ago, when the sun went down behind the red-clay bluffs of Maryland.

He shivered with excitement. He remembered what the captain of the *Erebus* had said: "I don't believe you can do much escaping in the bay." But he could! He knew he could!

"Mr. Key," he whispered, but Key didn't hear him. And Lex suddenly was glad he hadn't. If Lex said one word about escaping, it would make Lieutenant Key responsible—and maybe Colonel Skinner, too. Both of them had gone to meet the British Fleet under a flag of truce. Now they were prisoners. Their ship, stripped of its sails, was being towed by the *Surprise*.

Lex remembered how the angry colonel had accused the admiral of violating the flag of truce. But even if the admiral had done wrong, he thought, both Key and Skinner still intended to do what was right. They seemed to think it would be wrong for them to try to get away. If they knew that Lex was planning to escape, they might think that was wrong, too. They might even try to stop him. Lex decided to say nothing.

It would be easy to escape, he thought. He could crawl to an entry port, hang by his elbows, and drop quietly into the water. The west shore of the Chesapeake, where the signal fires were burning, couldn't be more than a mile away. Swimming that distance in the dark would be no risk at all.

But if he slipped away now, there was nothing he could

tell those men on the shore that they didn't know already. He couldn't tell them where the British troops were going to land. He had to wait until he knew. By that time, Lex thought, it would certainly be daylight.

Escaping in broad daylight would be dangerous. It might be impossible. If the British saw him swimming, a small boat could overtake him in no time at all. They might even shoot him in the water. But he was going to try.

The only thing that he could do, right now, was wait— and hope nobody on *Surprise* knew his parole was over.

In the gray twilight just before dawn, Lex lay down on the deck underneath the muzzle of a carronade. He curled up in the narrow space between the wooden gun truck and the bulwark and pretended to be fast asleep. He wouldn't be in anybody's way, he thought, but he would be in plain sight. It was better than to try to hide. Nobody would pay much attention to a sleeping boy.

He heard the sailors swarming up the hatchways from the lower decks. Without opening his eyes, he knew how they were piling their rolled hammocks into the hollow space between the two walls of thick planks that formed the bulwark. If a time came when he had to hide, that might be a good place. If he crawled underneath the top layer of the hammocks . . .

With all the noise of tramping feet around him, he went sound asleep.

The next thing Lex knew, a hand was jerking at his ankle.

He opened his eyes. Anyway, he tried to, but the lids were swollen. They felt hot and puffy.

"Landon!" The hand jerked again. "Wake up!" Lieutenant Key was squatting on the deck. "You've slept all day, with the sun beating on you. The soldiers have been packed so thick along the gangway that I didn't see you. You look as if you had been cooked. As a matter of fact, you've probably been better cooked than *this*. Here. . . ."

Key was holding out a sailor's mess pan. The handle of an iron spoon stuck up out of a brown, greasy stew.

"Maybe you can eat it," Key went on. "Colonel Skinner did. I couldn't." He had not shaved. His cheeks were covered with pale bristles, and his face looked even thinner than when Lex had seen him in the cabin of the *Tonnant*. "I wish I could sleep."

Lex sat up and reached out for the pan.

"Thank you," he said. The words came in a mumble. He felt awkward and embarrassed. What would the British think when they saw Key waiting on him? It would be another reason for them to make fun of the American militia. "You shouldn't have," Lex said. "You're . . . you're an officer."

"Don't worry about that." Key laughed—the same quick, angry, hopeless laugh that Lex had heard last night. "If a vice-admiral can send up flags about you, the way Cochrane did when he wanted you fetched from the *Erebus* to the *Tonnant*, a lieutenant can see that you get a bite of supper. Go ahead, now. Eat."

Lex tried. The stew tasted like sea water. It was made of brined beef, and it was so salty that one spoonful made his lips sting as if he had bitten nettles. Chewing the meat was like chewing splinters. The lumps of ship's biscuit crumbled in the grease were as hard as pebbles. But he had to eat. It wouldn't be good manners not to, after Mr. Key had gone to all that trouble.

"Where are we?" he asked, between spoonfuls.

"We passed Annapolis an hour ago." Key's face was grim. "You could see the people running. If you'd been awake, you could have. Wagons, coaches, gigs, carts— loaded with things they were trying to save. Women with big bundles on their backs."

"Like Alexandria," Lex said.

"Like Washington. Like Georgetown. I tried to send my wife away. She wouldn't go. Now the same thing is happening at Baltimore. I hope it's happening. The people ought to go. Cockburn swears he's going to burn the city."

"General Ross said he was going to keep his army there this winter."

"I know he did, but I've heard the soldiers talking. If the Jonathans fire one shot . . ."

"Jonathans?" It was a name Lex hadn't heard before.

"That's what the British call us. They say that if we dare to fight, the troops will be turned loose to plunder Baltimore before they burn it. They even hope we'll try to fight them, because that will give them an excuse to loot the city—to steal and smash things and hurt people who aren't soldiers, the same way they did at Hampton. They're so sure that they can whip us!"

"Can they?"

"I don't know. *I don't know!* All we have is a few little gunboats—rowboats with one gun apiece. A little brick fort in the harbor—Fort McHenry. And the same militia that they whipped three weeks ago. I don't want to think about it!" Mr. Key sprang up. "We'll know soon enough.

If the wind lasts, the whole fleet will be in the Patapsco River in the morning. By this time tomorrow, we'll know all about it."

Mr. Key was partly right. The next morning, the British Fleet was steering into the mouth of the river that led up to Baltimore, only fourteen miles away.

But Mr. Key was also partly wrong. Suddenly, the sails were furled. Anchors splashed in the brown water. The rumble of their cables running out was like the muttering of distant thunder. After that, the great fleet lay as quiet as if it had come to make a friendly visit. Hours went by, and still the three Americans on the *Surprise* knew nothing more than they had known the day before. They still did not know where Ross planned to land his army.

The seventy ships were stretched out in long lines across the river. The soldiers could go ashore on either bank. Or they could land on both sides of the river at the same time. There was no way to tell.

The ships were close together. For the first time, Lex could see the whole fleet plainly. There were four big line-of-battle ships with two long rows of gun ports, one above the other. There must be at least a dozen frigates. And he counted five of those queer-looking ships that carried the enormous, stubby mortars on their forward decks—the awful weapons that could hurl two-hundred-pound shells almost a mile into the sky.

The mortar ships were anchored in a row. The tide was ebbing, and their sterns had swung downstream. Lex could read their names—*Terror, Meteor* and *Devastation, Aetna* and *Volcano.*

The rails of all the vessels in the fleet were lined with men. They were loafing, gazing at the low shores and the cornfields and the patches of brown stubble where the grain already had been cut. All those thousands of men, talking, made a buzzing that reminded Lex of bees around the hives in the backyard at home on any long, hot, lazy afternoon.

Everything's so peaceful, Lex thought. It's so peaceful that it seems like Sunday. Then another thought surprised him: This is Sunday. This is the eleventh of September. He had been a prisoner for fourteen days. Two weeks ago today, the British came to Alexandria.

That Sunday had been very much like this one—hot and bright and peaceful. Lex remembered the neighbors standing on their front stoops, watching—the boys diving off the wharves and swimming out to get a closer look at the strange ships—the sailors waving at them, acting friendly. It hadn't seemed like war.

A few hours later, he had been in trouble. He had bored holes in the bottom of the *Lex and Robin,* and the enemy had caught him.

In a few hours, now, he might be in still worse trouble. He might be swimming, trying to escape. And the sailors and the soldiers on the ships would not be waving at him. If they saw him, they would probably be shooting.

It can't be very much worse, he told himself. It will be too dark for them to hit me. Or to catch me, either.

He hoped that he was right. He had made up his mind. As soon as the army started landing, he'd drop overboard. He'd swim up the river until he knew his strength was giving out—two miles, maybe three miles—before he went ashore. Then, if he were lucky, he would find a farmer who would let him have a horse. There must be farms, and barns with horses in them, on the road to

Baltimore. Even if he had to go all the way on foot, he was sure that he could travel faster than the British Army.

Lex was not afraid of what might happen to him. Not yet, anyway. He knew he would be, when the time came. The only thing that scared him now was what he heard the soldiers saying. They were packed along the bulwarks of the frigate in a solid red mass, pointing at the low shores of the river and making bets about where they would land. Some of them said it wouldn't make much difference. They said the Yankees had already run away.

Lex thought it might be true. There were no signs of life on either bank—no earthworks in the fields, no glitter of brass cannon.

A boy whose father was a major knew there ought to be scouts watching. There ought to be patrols of cavalry along the roads. But the two roads Lex could see were as empty as the fields. He stared at the underbrush along the edges of the distant woods, until his eyes ached from the glare of sun upon the river. Not a leaf stirred. Not one puff of dust rose up out of the woods to show that horsemen were on lookout duty where the roads were hidden by the trees.

Lex could hear the soldiers making jokes about it, laughing.

"Stupid Jonathans," he heard them saying. "Rabble. Cowardly clodhoppers. People that ain't got backbone enough to stand up for their country don't deserve to have one. Yuh! When we get done with 'em, they ain't goin' to have a country! It's ours, ain't it? Anyhow, it used to be. Well, then . . . We'll just take it back. That's what we came for, ain't it? Only thing is, it's too easy. Ain't no more excitement to it than there is to chasin' pigs out of a garden. Those Yankees run so fast that you can't even hear 'em squeal."

Lex felt his hands squeeze into fists. They squeezed so hard that drops of sweat oozed out between his fingers.

"You wait!" he said. But he didn't say it loud enough for anyone to hear. "We haven't run!" He tried to make himself believe it. "You just wait and see!"

Wait. . . . Wait. . . . Lex thought the day would never end.

At last the sun slid down until it touched the western hills. Its fierce glare turned the river as red as the soldiers' coats. The thin sliver of a new moon hung low in the sky for a few minutes. Then it, too, slid out of sight. One by one, the warships at both ends of the long, anchored lines became dim in the twilight. Darkness hid the row of mortar vessels. On the deck of the *Surprise,* Lex could not see even the tall masts soaring high above him. He could not see the fleet at all.

But he could hear it. And the noises that it made were different. Officers were giving orders. He could hear feet tramping and ropes squealing. There were bumps and thuds, and sounds of hurrying and jostling on the crowded decks.

Lex crouched underneath the barrel of a carronade and pressed his body tight against its wooden carriage.

The stars came out, bright in the cloudless sky. Their reflections in the water were almost as bright. They lighted up the river like a million winking candles. Lex could see, now, what the noises meant.

Sailors were piling cannon balls inside the round wooden hoops fastened to the deck beside each gun. Other sailors hauled on ropes, and small boats were swung across the bulwarks and let down into the water.

The soldiers were drawn up in ranks. They had their muskets, now. They had packs on their backs. At some of the places where the small boats had been lowered, Lex saw groups of sailors. They, too, carried muskets, and they had swords in their belts.

It wasn't just the British Army that was getting ready to attack the city! If *Surprise* was sending part of its crew ashore to help the soldiers, the other vessels in the fleet were probably doing the same thing.

Suddenly Lex felt as if an icy hand had pushed itself inside him. He could feel cold fingers squeezing at his stomach. There must be thousands upon thousands of sailors on these seventy ships. If even half of them joined with the army to attack the city, what chance would the militia have?

Mr. Key had been afraid the British Army, by itself, was so big the Americans could not stand up against it. But this was worse than anything that Francis Scott Key had imagined! It was something that the general at Baltimore should hear about as soon as possible. And Lex knew there was nobody else to take the warning to Sam Smith.

I'm still a soldier, he told himself. Captain Cutcheon never mustered out the Alexandria militia. I've got to get to Baltimore tonight. I've got to find General Smith and tell him. It's my duty. The idea that a boy who wasn't quite fifteen years old could be important made him feel less shaky. He couldn't be afraid. He *couldn't!*

And still there wasn't anything that he could do but

wait. It wouldn't be much help to the Americans to know about the sailors, if they didn't know which way the enemy was coming. Lex knew he couldn't help them by escaping, until he had found out whether the small boats, lying now along the ships' sides, were going to take the soldiers and the sailors to the north bank of the river or the south bank.

He'd never find out if he stayed here, hiding underneath the cannon.

The best place to hide and watch would be the frigate's bulwark. Usually, by this time of night, the sailors had taken their rolled hammocks out of the hollow space between the double wooden walls on both sides of this upper deck. But tonight, the hammocks were still there.

Could he pull himself up on the bulwark and crawl underneath a hammock without being seen? The starlight made the deck almost as bright as it would be in the gray twilight before dawn. But he had to take the risk.

He waited until half a dozen powder boys came climbing up a hatchway ladder from the magazine, deep down inside the ship. They ran toward the guns with armloads of cartridges that looked like bundles of cloth tightly sewed together. Lex jumped up and ran behind them.

He made for a place that he already had picked out, where the foremast and its rigging cast a kind of ghostly shadow on the bulwark. With one hand, he found the end of a rolled hammock. He lifted it a little, dragged himself up, and wriggled underneath it. He lay there, panting with excitement, hoping that the hammock covered him. It seemed to Lex that the hard hammering of his heart must certainly be making the canvas shake and quiver. If anybody walked along the gangway . . .

But nobody came. As the minutes went by, Lex felt better. Nobody had seen him crawl into his hiding place. The first part of his plan had worked!

He could hear the creak of leather belts, the clack of bayonets in their scabbards, the thud of a musket butt upon the deck, and a sergeant's angry mutter: "Quiet! Quiet, you!" The troops were moving. They were going down into the waiting boats. He could hear faint, pushing noises as oars shoved the boats away from the ship's side, and then the gurgle of the water as the oars dipped.

But he couldn't tell which way the boats were going. No matter how dangerous it was, he had to look. For all he knew, a sailor might be leaning on the bulwark right beside him, but that was another risk he had to take.

Slowly, carefully, he squirmed out from underneath the roll of canvas. He lay flat on the hammocks piled between the two walls of the bulwark, and peered down at the dark water of the river. It was glittering with stars. Here and there, the reflected starlight gleamed in sudden swirls and stretched out in pale streaks.

At last Lex knew what he had waited so long to find out!

The swirls were made by oar blades, and the streaks were the long ripples behind moving boats. All of them were going toward the north shore of the river!

The invading army was beginning to land on the low point where Lex had seen two dusty farm roads running across empty stubble fields and cornfields, until they disappeared into the woods.

Now was the time to drop overboard! Now!

He couldn't. There were too many boats. They came in ranks, like soldiers on parade. As soon as one mass of

small boats went by, another took its place. There seemed
to be no end to them.

Wait. . . . Wait. . . .

It was harder to wait, now, than ever. But Lex knew
that even a small splash would certainly be seen and
heard.

Every minute, he expected to be caught. Every muscle
in his body seemed to be pulled tight. He felt the cramps
beginning in his legs, as if he had been swimming for a
long time, instead of lying still. He felt the rolled-up
hammocks turning wet with dew.

Then the column of small boats was gone. There was
only the dark water, sprinkled with the motionless reflections of the stars. Now . . . !

Lex rolled over cautiously, until he felt the top edge
of the bulwark timber dig into his hip. His hands gripped
the wood, but it was damp and slippery with the dew. He
had meant to hang on for a moment and then drop feet
first into the river, so that he would make as little noise
as possible. Unfortunately, when he swung his body over
the ship's side, his fingers lost their hold. He fell as
clumsily and helplessly as a boy falling out of bed.

He tried to turn while he was falling. He pulled his
knees up to his stomach and flung out his arms to try to
twist his body. But there wasn't time.

The splash, he thought. They'll hear it. They can't
help but hear it. There was nothing he could do about
it. Yes, there is! Don't try to swim. Sink! *Sink!* The tide
will carry you a little way upstream, beyond the splash.

And then his left arm struck the sharp edge of an open
gun-port lid. A flash of pain exploded in his mind, and he
could think of nothing else.

The blow turned him over. He was face down when he hit the water, and his mouth was open.

He was choking, drowning. His surprise and fear made him forget about the splash, about the tide, about letting himself sink, about not trying to swim.

He struck out wildly with his arms and legs, and felt the sudden flash of pain again. It seemed to hit him, this time, in the face.

He got one gasp of air. And then, just as the water closed above his head the second time, he saw the sheen of the wet oar blade that had struck his cheek, and the dim shape of a longboat sliding slowly past him.

Chapter 8

ONE ARM BROKEN, AND THE OTHER TIED

Fingers twisted themselves into Lex's hair. They dragged him up out of the river. He could breathe again. They dragged him in across the gunwale of the longboat. He could feel the gunwale scrape his chest. He could feel the buttons being torn off his shirt.

He slid into the boat.

The fingers gripping his hair jerked him to his knees. He was facing two men sitting on the stern thwart of the longboat. They were sailors; he could see the flat brims of their hats. He heard one of them say:

"Swelp me! It's that bantam rooster of a Yankee that was on the *Erebus* some days ago. Fell overboard from that there frigate we just passed. He must have. What in thunder are we goin' to do about him?"

"Fetch him along." The other sailor sounded angry.

"We're not wastin' time to put him back on board. If we're any later, the admiral will have the cat across our backs. Give way, you men. Lay into those oars! Pull!"

The fingers let go. Lex slumped down. He felt the long-boat surge ahead.

The wet-mud, fishy smell of tide flats came into his nose. Tall, rustling stems of swamp reeds brushed the gunwales. The keel of the longboat made a hushing sound in soft muck and then grated on coarse gravel. From the shore, Lex heard a murmured question:

"What boat's that?"

"Number 46, sir," the man at the tiller muttered. "From *Erebus*, sir. Landin' party. Twenty seamen." He whispered to the sailor on the thwart beside him. "Take this Yankee cockerel with you. I got to make another trip. I got to go back for twelve hundredweight of rockets, an' I ain't got time to bother with no prisoner. I ain't got time to answer questions about how we got him, neither. Keep ahold of him. Don't let him sneak away."

The murmur came from the dark shore again:

"Out with you, men. Form on the beach. Join up with the naval brigade. It's on top of the bank, about thirty yards ahead."

Men sprang out into the shallow water. The sailor on the stern thwart reached for Lex's arm. He yelped with pain.

"Quiet, you!" the voice on shore said. "D' you want to bring the Yankees on us? Do that again, I'll quiet you!"

"He'll do it, too," the sailor whispered. "Keep your tongue behind your teeth unless you want 'em knocked out. I'm just goin' to tie you up so I'll know where you are."

"The other arm," Lex mumbled. "That one hurts."

"A' right. Port or starboard, it's all one to me."

Lex felt a rope tied tight around his right wrist. It dragged him up. It pulled his arm straight out. The sailor, jerking the rope, hauled him across the gunwale. He splashed into knee-deep water that grew shallower. His feet sank into sand.

All around him, in the darkness, he heard the swish of other feet, the clack of cutlasses, the grunt of men, the hss-ssh of heavy loads dropped on the beach.

There was a high bank ahead. Dry grass rasped against his legs. He stumbled over a man lying down, and the man called him a bad name in a whisper.

"A' right," the sailor said. "Down with you. No tricks, neither. I'm keepin' ahold of this here rope."

Lex lay down. He spent the rest of the night lying in the thick, dew-soaked grass, with men all around him.

There wasn't much of the night left. In the twilight before sunrise, he saw that he was in the midst of a mass of sailors in blue jackets. But that wasn't all. The fields that had been empty Sunday afternoon were filled with troops in scarlet coats. Some of them were standing in ranks, leaning on their muskets. Others lay in a long skirmish line that faced the woods. Seeing them, Lex knew the British really weren't sure that the Americans weren't going to fight. It made him feel good, for a minute.

But there were so many soldiers—solid, red blocks of them. There were cannon, too. He counted eight, and some were field guns like the ones he'd seen on the Potomac shore, except that these were bigger; and some were short and stubby like the dreadful mortars on the bomb ships. There were ammunition carts, and other carts with the long sticks of rockets in them. And even in the dark, the British somehow had unloaded horses from the ships to haul the cannon.

How could the American militia fight these thousands of trained soldiers? And the cannon and the rockets and the swarm of sailors?

All of his fine plans for warning the Americans had failed. It made him sick to think how he'd been caught not more than half a minute after he had tried to get away. Now he was tied up like a hound-dog on a leash. The fierce pain in his arm was getting worse. It was making him feel even sicker.

The sailor who was holding the rope tied to Lex's wrist sat up and yawned. Then he looked at the boy.

"What's the matter, Yankee? I'm not goin' to kill you. If you get killed, it'll be some other Yankee does it, when the shootin' starts." The sailor sounded cheerful. "Nothin' to worry about. Sa-ay, how'd you do that? Your left arm is swelled up like a sausage." He nudged the seaman next to him. "Pass the word for the surgeon's mate."

A pock-faced young man, with a bundle under his elbow, strolled across the field. He squatted down and poked at Lex's swollen wrist.

"Broken," he said. "Nice, clean break. Pretty . . . pretty. He's not ours, though. Where'd you get him?"

"Prisoner," the sailor said. "But he's a bit of all right. He helped one of our marines when he was wounded."

"Can't waste splints on Yankees. Scratch 'round in the grass and find some sticks. Aye, that'll do. Now hold him, some of you; he's going to wriggle like a worm in a ship's biscuit."

Sparks of pain shot up through Lex's arm, but the sailors didn't have to hold him. He wouldn't give them a new reason for believing that Americans were cowards. He wouldn't let them know how much it hurt. He *wouldn't!* And he didn't. He couldn't keep the tears from running down his cheeks, but he did not move while the surgeon's mate pulled at his wrist, wound a bandage tight around three crooked, dirty sticks, and made a sling to go around his neck.

"There . . . you've had your battle, boys. This here is probably the only wounded Yankee you'll see all day," the pock-faced man said. "The rest will run too fast."

The sailor slapped Lex on the shoulder.

"Hurt, huh?" he asked. Lex shook his head. "Tell you what I'll do. You just pass your word, man to man like, not to cut an' run, an' I'll untie this rope."

"No!" Lex said.

"It'll likely jerk you, when we get to movin'."

"*No!*" Lex said it again, stubbornly.

"A' right. Have it your own way. Lookee, now . . . we're movin' out already."

The soldiers who had been lying in a long skirmish line across the fields were falling into column in the road. A drum rolled suddenly. It sounded to Lex like an empty barrel tumbling down an endless flight of wooden steps. At the signal, the red-coated soldiers began marching.

They marched as if they were made out of wood. Their legs moved like the pendulums of clocks.

Lex saw a group of officers on horseback ride across a stubble field and stop beside the road to watch the troops go by.

Two of them looked familiar. He had seen both of them somewhere. He had seen them more than once!

The last time, they'd been sitting at the table in the cabin of the *Tonnant*. One of them was General Ross. The man in the blue coat, beside him, was Admiral Cockburn. But the first time he had seen them, they had been on horses. They had been riding up the dusty street in Washington.

There was something different about the general today. No . . . not about the general himself. About his horse. He was riding a different horse today.

The scarlet regiment disappeared into the woods. Somewhere, close by, there was a sudden twittering—a peep . . . peep-peep.

"There goes the bosun's pipe," the sailor said. He tugged the rope on Lex's arm. "Here we go. They're puttin' us right close up front."

The mass of seamen started up the road. There were a lot of them. The naval brigade, drawn from seventy ships, was bigger than the whole regiment ahead.

But it didn't march like soldiers. Lex thought it marched like American militia. Its muskets stuck out every which way. Some sailors carried them strapped to their backs; some held them by the muzzles, upside down; some tucked them underneath their arms, slanting, the way hunters did.

All the seamen acted as if they were going on a picnic. They shouted and sang songs. They shoved and jostled. When they saw bunches of wild grapes on the vines hanging from the trees, they broke out of the column and went plunging through the underbrush to pick them.

Their racket filled the woods. Lex couldn't hear the other regiments at all. When he looked back, though, they were coming in stiff, silent ranks that filled the country road from side to side.

The road made a kind of tunnel through the woods. The trees met overhead. At first, it was cool and pleasant in the tunnel, but after a few miles, the day turned hot. The tramping feet stirred up the dust. Lex felt it gritting on his teeth. With one arm in a sling and the other fastened to a jerking rope, he couldn't rub the dirt out of his eyes.

Behind, there was a sudden rush of noise. The weeds along the roadside smoked with dust. They crackled as if they were burning. Horses' legs were breaking the dry, brittle stems.

General Ross on his white horse came riding by, going toward the head of the long column. Admiral Cockburn and a bugler and a dozen officers and orderlies rode with him.

They raised a choking cloud that rolled in waves across the marching sailors. Men coughed and muttered. The blue sleeve of the sailor who held Lex's rope turned reddish brown with dirt. Lex could hardly see three ranks ahead of him. He began to think again about escaping. Maybe he could jerk the rope loose. Maybe he could dive into the underbrush. The dust might hide him. He began to watch for a good place to try it.

But he was in the middle of the column. There were two men on one side of him, and three men on the other. And there were soldiers in the woods on both sides of the road. He could hear the threshing noises of the flank patrols. He could hear feet scuffling in dry leaves and dead sticks breaking and the sound of vines and brambles tearing.

And the woods were getting thinner.

Wait, Lex told himself. You've got to wait. It seemed to him that he'd been doing nothing else for days. There'll be a better place.

Before he found it, the trees ended. Rail fences ran beside the road. Lex saw a barnyard and a water trough. He saw stables and a pigsty and a long, low chicken house. In a weedy yard, there was a small white farmhouse with a porch in front. The farmhouse roof came down over the porch. It made Lex think of the brim of a boy's cap, pulled low over his eyes.

The little yard was full of horses. An orderly was walking the general's white horse back and forth.

Chairs and a table, taken from the house, stood in the brown, tramped grass near the front step. There were dishes on the table, and a red-and-white checked cloth. The general and the admiral were eating breakfast.

The regiment ahead was halted in the road. Now the naval brigade also stopped. The sailors were not interested in Ross and Cockburn. But they, too, were hungry; they saw pigs rooting in the barnyard; and they saw chickens scratching. They began to yell. The blue column came to pieces. In a minute, hundreds of seamen were swarming over the rail fences, chasing pigs and chickens.

"Lookee, Yank," the sailor holding Lex's rope said. "Don't seem like it's right that I should miss my dinner on account of you. Any chicken that you catch, I'll give you half. Let's see what's inside that henhouse."

The rope pulled Lex's arm straight out in front of him. He had to run to keep from falling down.

Other sailors were already in the chicken house. It was dark there, and the air was full of feathers. Hens flew from roost to roost with frightened squawks and ran between the sailors' legs. The seamen made blind grabs to catch them, and then whooped with laughter when they caught each other instead of the chickens.

I'll never have another chance like this, Lex thought. He jerked the rope out of the sailor's hand, ducked underneath a slanting roost of poles, and ran for the small patch of sunlight he saw at the far end of the shed.

The sailor shouted and came after him, but the others were having so much fun that they didn't realize their prisoner had broken loose. They thought that this was part of the exciting game of catch-your-dinner. Two of them pretended that the man chasing Lex was one of the squawking hens. They made a dash for him and clutched him, and all three of them went sprawling. They were still rolling on the dirt floor when Lex reached the streak of daylight that came through a doorway.

The streak was not much wider than a crack. The door was almost closed.

And it wouldn't open.

When Lex pushed, the bottom of it scraped the ground. It stuck.

More yells burst out behind him. They sounded different now. The seamen had stopped laughing. They could see him struggling with the door.

He threw all his weight against it.

The bottom still stuck, but the boards were springy. They bent a little. The door leaned outward at the top.

Lex used his shoulder as a wedge. He pushed it into the narrow space to keep the boards from springing back.

The door was squeezing him. The rough edge scraped his chest where the skin already had been scraped raw when he was dragged in across the gunwale of the long-boat.

He raised one leg and got his knee against the boards and made the crack a little wider. Feet were pounding toward him as he wriggled out.

The barnyard was an uproar of squealing pigs and whooping men. Lex dodged behind a straw stack . . . then behind a corncrib . . . then around the corner of a sagging shed with an old wagon in it.

Tall nettles grew behind the shed. Lex felt them sting his face as he plunged into them. He didn't care. He'd done it! He had *almost* done it!

Across a cornfield, where the stalks still stood in rows, he saw thick woods. He headed for the shelter of the trees at a dead run.

And then, between the dry stalks of the corn, he saw the scarlet regiment still halted in the road. It was close . . . close! The road curved around the cornfield in a sharp bend, and some of the soldiers were so close that they could throw a clod of dirt at him and hit him. They were leaning on their muskets, watching the antics of the sailors in the farmyard.

But one of them raised his arm and pointed at the running boy. Then he raised his musket.

Lex swerved away. The hard ridges of the corn rows tripped his feet. The hard edges of the dead leaves raked his face. At every step, he expected the roar of the musket. He expected the whufff-mmm of a bullet, or a hard blow on his back. If the big ball from a British musket hit him, he would never hear it. He could feel the place where it was going to hit him. The place was on the right side of his backbone, just above his belt. It was a peculiar, numb feeling. The imaginary place felt cold and tight.

The shot didn't come. All he heard was the tearing sound of brittle corn leaves slashing at his clothes, and the tearing sound of his own breath.

He was breathing in hard gasps that hurt. His arm, hanging in its sling, bumped on his ribs.

He didn't care. The open field was ending. The woods were just ahead.

A tangled mat of wild-cucumber vines clung to his legs. He waded through it. Thick underbrush rose like a hedge to stop him. He put up his good arm to shield his face, and plunged on through the whipping branches.

And then he was in the hot, dim twilight of the oak woods. The ground was level. It was covered with a carpet of last year's dead leaves. Old acorns crunched beneath his feet. Dead twigs snapped. In the quiet woods, the little sounds were loud.

Lex stopped. He listened. When he wasn't running, there were no sounds at all. He had really done it! He had got away!

The pain was burning in his broken wrist. Hot sparks were shooting up again into his shoulder. His lungs burned, too, and the sparks seemed to be inside him, in his chest.

He wanted to lie down. He wanted to lie on the soft carpet of dry leaves and rest for hours. No . . . years.

Lex knew he couldn't rest for even a few minutes. He was still a soldier. He was still a part of that poor little company of Alexandria militia. And he had a duty. There was still a chance for him to get to Baltimore in time. Every minute was important.

He slipped the sling over his head and tore it with his teeth and twisted the torn ends around his belt. He tied them as tight as he could, to keep his wrist from bumping.

Then he began to run again.

Chapter 9

THE GENERAL'S LAST RIDE

LEX listened to the sound of his own feet. It was quick and crisp at first . . . ksshh . . . ksshh . . . on the matted leaves.

Every time he heard it, he knew there was one less step he'd have to take.

It was a good thing to know. Every step was sending a hard jolt of pain up through his arm.

The sound was changing now. It was a kind of slow swusshh, a wait, and then a swusshh again.

His feet dragged. They were scuffling the dead leaves. Two, three times, he stumbled. He hadn't run more than two miles yet, and Baltimore must be at least five miles away. Or six miles. Maybe seven. But he was getting tired already.

He hadn't slept a wink for two nights. He had been awake ever since Lieutenant Key fetched him the pan of brined-beef stew on the deck of the *Surprise*. That had been along about the middle of the afternoon on Saturday. This was Monday.

The insides of his legs were quivering. His feet were getting heavier. It was harder, every step, to lift them. That burst of running through the cornfield, thinking every moment he was going to be shot, had taken something out of him.

A bugle blatted. Then another and another. A long way behind him, so faint he could hardly hear them, the drums of the British infantry began to roll.

Lex knew what that meant. The army was advancing once more. All the scarlet regiments, the thousand sailors, the cannon and the rocket carts were coming up the road again. He tried to make himself run faster.

Suddenly, he knew it didn't matter.

A rifle shot cracked in the woods ahead.

Ahead!

He had been so sure that all the British were behind him, and he had been wrong. While the general and the admiral were eating breakfast, back there in the front yard of the farmhouse, the advance guard had been far in front.

A dozen more shots cut the air like whips. They made Lex think of times in Alexandria when big, canvas-topped freight wagons lined the waterfront, and the loafing drivers tried to pull each other's hats off with the crackling lashes of their long whips.

Lex felt as if he'd been a fool, this morning and last night.

He had thought that he was so important. Now he knew that everything he'd done was useless—throwing himself off the frigate's bulwark, breaking his arm, escaping from the sailors, running to tell the Americans which way the enemy was coming.

They hadn't needed any warning. They'd known, all along, about the British Army.

They hadn't run away. They hadn't even waited for the invading army to attack the city. They'd marched out to meet it.

And now they were fighting!

The British troops were shooting back at them. The loud explosions of their muskets sounded like the blows of iron mauls pounding on boards, smashing the boards into kindling.

Lex couldn't see the redcoats, but their firing line was close. It wasn't a line really. It was only a few men scattered in the underbrush where the woods ended, fifty yards ahead. He could see the spurts of dirty-gray smoke swelling out and hanging low above the bushes.

Something went splutt! in the dry leaves just in front of him. Another rifle bullet whickered past his head.

Lex was in the middle of a battle—on the wrong side.

Any moment, one of those stray rifle balls might hit him, but he couldn't go back. If he did, he would soon be a prisoner again.

He couldn't stay here either. There were more troops in the woods behind him. Already, he could hear the British signal whistles shrilling.

Lex ran on toward the lumps of powder smoke that lay like giant toadstools on the underbrush.

The slam-banging of the big Tower muskets was close,

now. It was much closer than it ought to be. *It was coming toward him.*

Only a few yards ahead, he saw a man in a short scarlet jacket running. Other men came thrashing through the bushes. They dodged from tree to tree. Their mouths were open, panting.

Lex stopped and stood staring at them. He could not believe what he was seeing.

The British were retreating!

He knew that this was only the beginning of the battle. These few men, running to the rear, were only part of the advance guard. But they had met American militia, and the Americans were winning this first fight!

All but one of the red-coated skirmishers had disappeared. The soldier just in front of Lex was trying to push his way through a blackberry thicket. Long vines coiled around him. The thorns were ripping at his jacket. They were pulling his white crossbelt out of place, until the big brass buckle that should be in front, below his chest, was underneath his arm. He was so close that Lex could see the shiny trickles of sweat on his face.

The soldier raised his musket.

For a moment, he seemed to be looking straight at Lex.

But he held the gleaming barrel of the musket with one hand. With the other hand, he took off his black-leather cap. He mopped his wet forehead with his sleeve and put the cap on again. He pushed one finger down inside the high, tight collar of his jacket, trying to loosen it. Then, slowly, he turned around. Lex was looking at the heavy knapsack on his back and the white cartridge box above his hip. The cartridge box was crooked.

Another rifle shot slashed at the woods.

The soldier's polished black cap tipped slowly backward and slid down his neck. Still holding his musket in his hands, the soldier leaned forward a little. As if the long lash of a whip that knocked his cap off had wrapped itself around his head and was pulling him, he leaned over slowly . . . farther . . . farther . . . until he disappeared among the vines. Only the empty cap lay on the tangled brambles, bouncing slowly.

It was hard for Lex to realize that he had seen a man shot.

This wasn't what he had imagined war was like—a few puffs of smoke, a few men bobbing up out of the underbrush like red-painted jumping jacks and hurrying away, and one man all alone, waist-deep in a blackberry thicket, falling as quietly as if he had decided to lie down and sleep.

Lex couldn't see a sign of the Americans. He looked around and couldn't see the British soldiers either. He hadn't realized, until now, that the British fought like Indians, hiding behind trees and crouching in the bushes. But they were there behind him. He could see the flashes of their muskets. And the Americans were in the edges of the woods ahead. The whipcracks of the rifle shots were louder.

Lex was between the skirmish lines of the two armies!

He heard a quick tap on the tree beside him. It was no louder than the rap of a woodpecker's bill. But when he looked, he saw a brownish-white streak where a bullet had plowed a furrow in the bark.

Lex threw himself face down.

He hit the ground with his hurt arm underneath him. But he couldn't stop to think about the pain. The bramble thicket was only a few feet away. He rolled over on his side and wriggled toward it.

There was an opening among the vines—a kind of cave between old, woody stalks, with the new growth of the summer arching over it. Instead of dry leaves, there was grass here. It was long and green in the shade of the blackberry tangle. It made no sound at all as Lex dragged himself along.

He felt safer. Occasionally, he could hear the sound of bullets. He could even tell which were American and which were British. The musket balls made a sound like a man gargling. The rifle bullets whined; they seemed to pull a long, thin string of sound behind them. But all of them were three or four feet above the ground.

The cave through the thicket turned and twisted. Lex was not sure which way he was going. Before he knew it, the woods ended. The bramble patch pushed out into a meadow. The grass was brown there.

He lay underneath the vines and looked across the brown grass. Off to the right a little way, he saw the yellowy-red road. The road was empty. Ahead, there were a few big oak trees and a few low bushes. Then there was a rail fence and another piece of meadow and then woods again.

Beyond the fence, a big, lumpy man in a gray-blue coat was sitting on a horse as calmly as if he didn't know there was a battle. He was the first American Lex had seen since the firing started. The boy felt his throat go tight with fear for that brave man out there in the open meadow, with no shelter, where the enemy could see him plainly. Yet he felt proud, too. The British said that the Americans were cowards!

A long, straight streak of smoke jumped out from one of the big oaks, not more than twenty yards away. Lex saw a rifle barrel slide back out of sight behind the trunk. The American militiamen were fighting in that narrow strip of trees and bushes, with the fence behind them! He saw a sleeve, almost the color of the smoke, jerk up and down. He even heard the scraping of the ramrod as the soldier drove another bullet down the barrel of his rifle.

Suddenly, he couldn't hear it. A musket slammed. Half a dozen of them went off, almost together. They were so close around him that the crashes hit his ears like fists.

The British skirmishers had stopped retreating. They were coming back! And there were more of them now.

As Lex watched, the Americans gave way. A dozen men sprang up out of the bushes. Others darted from behind trees. They wore white crossbelts, like the British, but their coats were pale blue. So were their caps. The caps looked as big as buckets. They had chin straps that hung down like the handle of a bucket upside down. They had feathers that stuck up in front.

The feathers looked as if they'd come out of the tails of roosters. They fluttered as the militiamen ran toward the fence and scrambled over it or crawled between the rails.

Not all of the Americans were trying to escape. Two of those who'd started for the fence had turned around again. They were running toward the enemy! It seemed to Lex that they were running straight toward him. Then they ducked out of sight behind the same trees where they had been hiding. For just a second, Lex had seen their faces.

They weren't men! They were only boys!

Their faces, squeezed between their chin straps and the black, shiny visors of their bucket-shaped caps, made Lex think of the young marine aboard the British rocket ship. They weren't much older. They weren't much older than the boys in the Alexandria militia company—the boys who'd been sent home because they were too young, because there weren't enough of them to stand up to the enemy.

There were only two of these boys. And they didn't seem to know they were too young, any more than Joe Piery had known he was too old. Like Piery, they were standing up to the whole British Army!

They were steadying the barrels of their rifles on the rough bark of the oak trees. They were taking aim. The rifles pointed toward the road.

The road wasn't empty, now. The piece of it that Lex could see had filled up suddenly with scarlet uniforms— with men on horseback, and a solid column of red-coated infantry behind them.

The officer in front, on the white horse, was General Ross.

Lex felt as if he had been here before. It was a queer feeling.

The country road wasn't like the street in Washington where he had watched the ranks of British soldiers flowing toward him. There weren't any houses. There weren't any picket fences with tall gateposts, and the gates chained shut. There wasn't any dried-up, wrinkled little man in dirty overalls, wanting to fight the British by himself.

But Lex had a feeling that something he had seen before was happening again.

It is a feeling that often comes to soldiers in a war.

What happened was almost the same. Not quite.

There were two shots instead of one.

This time the general's horse did not rear back on its hind legs and topple over. The general did not leap off, alert and quick, giving orders instantly. He just sat there. His mouth opened, but no sound came out. He didn't look as if he had been hit. He only looked surprised.

And then, like a man so drowsy that he couldn't hold his head up any longer, he slumped in the saddle, and his chin sagged down between the gold-laced points of his high collar.

His hands lost the reins. They hung, swinging loosely, on the neck of the white horse. His fingers touched the hilt of the sword at his belt and slipped off. Then his hand, too, was swinging loosely.

As if that empty, dangling hand was so heavy that it made him lose his balance, Ross fell toward it.

Another mounted officer rode up beside him and threw out one arm to catch him, but the general was heavy. For a moment, his head lay on the officer's shoulder. Then his right leg dragged across the saddle, and he kept on falling. He slid downward, out of sight, the way the soldier in the bramble patch had slowly disappeared.

The general's body, crumpled in the road, was hidden by a thicket of legs in black gaiters.

For a minute then—or maybe half a minute, or two minutes—the same things that had happened in the street in Washington kept happening all over again. Officers were shouting. Lex could see their mouths wide open. He could even see their tongues move as they bellowed orders.

Their tongues looked pale pink in the middle of their red, sun-scalded faces.

Officers on foot and horseback waved their arms and pointed with their swords. This time the swords all pointed in the same direction—toward the oak trees where the two Americans were hiding. Soldiers began to break away from the neat ranks of the British column. They rushed past the group of men who crouched and knelt around the body of the general. They leaned forward as they ran. Their long, broad, three-edged bayonets flashed like slanting spearheads in the sun.

Some of them stopped waist-deep in the thickets. Others dropped to one knee in the brown grass of the meadow. All the lifted bayonets and gleaming musket barrels came down, level. The muskets went off like a single shot. A wave of dirty smoke rolled toward the oaks.

The trees no longer sheltered the two riflemen. One was running, with his back turned. The rolling smoke wave didn't reach him, but he plunged headfirst into the bushes as if it had pushed him. The other American was reloading, and he had forgotten to be careful. Half his jacket was in plain sight. The musket ball that hit him turned him all the way around before he fell.

The British soldiers yelled. Through their hoarse cries, Lex could hear the clatter of their ramrods as they pushed fresh charges down their musket barrels. One by one, and then by twos and threes, they began to run toward the rail fence.

There were only three Americans left now in the whole meadow. One of them was sitting on the fence, with one leg thrown over the top rail and a black boot swinging while he poured powder into the pan of his long rifle. Just behind him, a man whose sleeve was almost covered by the broad, black chevrons of a sergeant was crouching on his knees and one hand, just as he had fallen when he jumped the fence. A little farther back, the big man on the bay horse was still sitting calmly in his saddle. Both he and the sergeant were staring at the tall, slim figure on the fence. The red-coated skirmishers were lunging toward them, but those three men did not move.

Lex wanted to scream at them: "Run! *Run!*" But he knew that it would do no good. They were not going to run.

Instead, the dangling black boot was pushed down until its toe hooked underneath the bottom rail. Lex saw quick gleams of sunlight twitching on the long gold fringes of an epaulet. The young man with the rifle was a lieutenant, risking his life to give his sergeant time to get away.

The long barrel came up. With the butt still not quite at his shoulder, the lieutenant looked down at the kneeling sergeant. Lex heard his voice, clear, steady:

"Time to go, MacKensie. I can't stay here all day." And then, sharper, clearer: "Go on, Mac!"

The sergeant heaved himself up on his feet, but he did not go. He just stood there, shaking his head stubbornly. The nearest bayonets were not ten yards away. It seemed to Lex that they were reaching for those two brave men, almost touching them already.

Suddenly the bayonets stopped moving. A dozen British soldiers threw their muskets to their shoulders.

Lex saw the quick, thin smoke spurt from the rifle muzzle. But he did not hear the quick, thin spurt of sound that should have come at the same time. The crash of the big muskets smothered it. The fence was blotted out by their thick smoke. It clung to the rails and drifted slowly upward. As it wisped away, he saw that the fence was empty. He saw, beyond the rails, two blue-gray splotches on the brown grass. One of them lay still. The other jerked a little.

Lex felt an awful sickness rising in his throat. He had been afraid, in Washington, when he thought the house was burning and he was trapped in it. He had been afraid when he was locked in the dark cell on board the *Erebus,* and when the American shore batteries were smashing the bulwarks and cutting the tarred ropes of the ratlines to which he was clinging.

He had been afraid time and again. But not like this! He knew, now, what fear was.

This wasn't a real battle. It was just a skirmish. But within ten minutes, he had seen six men shot. He'd seen General Ross die—and the two boys who had killed him die a minute later. They were brave, he thought. They were so brave. They're dead. It could have been me, that day in Washington. If I hadn't run when Piery told me to . . . If I'd stayed and fought, like those two boys, I would be dead. I would have died three weeks ago. And then he thought, I'm going to die today.

His hand pushed deeply into the matted grass. His fingers dug into the soft earth underneath. They tried to hold the earth. They twisted themselves into the tough roots of the grass as if they were trying to keep him here, safe, in his hiding place. He tried to tell himself that he was really safe. I am. I am! All I've got to do is stay here.

Suddenly, Lex Landon knew why he was now so terribly afraid. He knew he couldn't stay!

The American Army was out there, somewhere, in the woods ahead. And he knew he had to find it.

The warning he had tried so hard to bring was useless. But there was something else now that could be important —maybe even more important!

The Baltimore militiamen had lost this first fight with the British, but they didn't know what really happened. They don't know about Ross, Lex was thinking. There's no way for them to know, unless I tell them. I'm the only one left, now. That man on horseback couldn't see Ross shot; the woods were in the way. I've got to tell them. Even if I'm killed, I've got to try. I've got to! But his fingers still clung to the twisted grass roots. I can't do it! I'm not brave. I don't want to be brave! I don't want to be killed.

Lex pressed his face down hard against the ground and let the sickness come. . . .

When he could raise his head again, he didn't want to look at what he saw over in the meadow.

The red-coated skirmishers still stood where they had fired that dreadful volley. He could see their ramrods working.

And the big American on horseback, all alone now in the meadow, was riding calmly toward them.

Close to the fence, he swung down from the saddle. Without even glancing at the British soldiers a few yards away, he bent over the two bodies in the grass. He knelt. He picked up one of them. Lex saw him stagger with its weight, but he carried it to the horse and dumped it like a sack of meal across the saddle. There were black chevrons on the dangling arms.

With one hand clutching the unconscious sergeant's

sleeve and the other holding the reins, he turned the horse and walked beside it slowly . . . slowly . . . back across the meadow.

Lex felt the sickness rising up in him again. It was different this time. He was sick with shame at his own selfish thoughts and at his fear.

A musket shot slammed out. Another. And another. But they missed. The woods closed in around the horse; the broad, blue-gray shoulders disappeared. A whistle shrilled. The British skirmishers began to climb the fence. They spread out into a thin, crooked line and trotted toward the woods.

The boy's clenched fingers loosened their grip on the wadded lump of grass roots. His fingers felt numb, and they were dirty, slippery with the earth that his sweat had turned to mud. He wiped them on his pants. Then he squirmed around in the low, brambly tunnel and began to crawl. He had told himself he couldn't leave this safe place. Now he was doing it, and it seemed almost easy. He was still afraid, but not the way he had been.

Behind him, on the road, a bugle blatted. It was close— so close that his whole body jerked. His lips began to twitch. He turned his head and pressed his mouth against his arm to make the twitching stop. And then, suddenly, he realized that it wasn't the weak quivering of fear. It was the beginning of a grin! He was grinning at a silly idea that had jumped into his mind: That bugle sounds exactly like a scared calf bawling. The foolish thought was followed by another: It sounds exactly like Joe Piery squawking at me.

Far away, another bugle squawked. Then three, four more joined in. They sounded like a whole pastureful of

noisy calves. They sounded like a whole crowd of dried-
up little old men yelling. They reminded Lex of Piery's
funny way of talking.

Grits and gravy! he thought. Why . . . why . . . something's happened to me! I'm all right! I must be, getting
crazy notions like that! I'm going to be all right!

What had happened to Lex Landon, in the last few
minutes, was that he had turned into a soldier.

He crawled on through the winding tunnel. It wasn't
easy. When he scrooched down underneath the lowest
branches of the berry brambles, his broken wrist dragged
on the ground. When he humped his back to lift the wrist,
tied to his belt, the long thorns gouged through his shirt
and dug into his skin. But he kept on going.

The squawking of the bugles stopped. A drum began
to growl. All up and down the road, the other British
drums took up the deep, harsh sound. They made a rapid,
rolling thunder like the rumble of wheels rolling over
loose planks of a bridge, with the iron hoofs of galloping
horses pounding on the planks at the same time.

That's good, Lex thought. That's fine. It doesn't matter
how much noise I make now. They can't hear me in that
racket.

He crawled faster. When thorns snagged his shirt, he
didn't stop to wriggle himself loose; he ripped his way
through without worrying about the noise.

His hand came down on something cold and hard. Its
sharp edge hurt. He pulled back his hand and saw a long,
dull gleam of steel. A musket lay there in the grass. Its
butt was hidden in the vines, but he had put his hand
down on the lock, and the sharp flint in its jaws had dug
into his palm. It gave him a peculiar feeling—not scared

exactly, but not pleasant either. This must be the place where the British soldier had been shot while he was tugging at his twisted crossbelt. The dead soldier must be lying right here, not more than two or three feet away.

Lex slid the musket along the grass, until the butt caught on a vine. The vines shook. Something came tumbling down. It made a soft bump on the musket barrel. It rolled a little and lay still, and Lex was looking at a black-leather cap. The last time he had seen that shiny cap, it was bouncing on the limber green tips of the vines.

He peered into the thicket. There, so close that he could almost touch it, was a limp hand with a scarlet cuff above it. The soldier's arm was underneath one end of the white cartridge box at which he had been tugging just before he fell.

I want that cartridge box. Lex didn't want to touch the soldier, but he did. He found the buckle of the crossbelt and unfastened it and dragged the belt away. The paper cartridges in the white-leather box made a small, whispering sound. The bayonet made little clickings in its scabbard.

Lex pushed his arm through one loop of the crossbelt. He gripped the barrel of the musket and began to crawl again. He slid the musket ahead, a few inches at a time, and hitched himself along. Slide . . . hitch. Slide the musket . . . pull one knee forward . . . pull the other knee up. It was slow work. It was too slow. Lex took a deep breath and stood up.

When his head and shoulders were clear of the brambles, he saw that he had crawled almost to the end of the blackberry thicket.

The long rolling of the drums had stopped. It had

turned into quick, separate thuds. Thud. Thud. Thud
. . . thud . . . thud. The British Army had begun to march
again. The drums were beating time.

Lex went thrashing through the last of the clinging
vines. He laid the musket on the rustling dry leaves at
his feet, and buckled on the belt. Then he picked up the
gun. It was heavy, but when his fingers fitted themselves
around the thick bulge underneath the wooden stock,
balanced perfectly. Hanging in his hand, with his arm
straight down beside his leg, the long barrel was parallel
with the ground. It stayed that way when he began to run.

He ran until the thudding of the drums was so faint he
could hardly hear it. Then he turned to the right, toward
Baltimore and toward the place where the American
Army must be waiting. He used the distant bumping of
the British drums to guide him.

Chapter 10

A LOST RACE AND A LAST CHANCE

Lex didn't know how long he had been running. He didn't know how far he'd come. But the drums were keeping up with him.

It seemed to Lex that their thud-thud . . . thud-thud-thudder was in front of him, now. He began to worry.

He couldn't understand how soldiers marching in a column could move faster than he had been running. It must be that the trees and underbrush and the low, swampy places in the woods were making him lose time. Circling around them, dodging them, he had to travel farther than the soldiers on the road.

His heart was pounding like the drums. It was even louder. His gasping breath was louder than the dry sounds that his feet made on the dead leaves, and his mouth was drier than the leaves.

The woods began to change. The oaks were bigger, not so close together. Lex caught a glimpse of sky.

He burst through a fringe of sumacs and slim, springy poplar saplings, and the sudden uproar of the drums burst on his ears like an explosion.

The British Army was ahead of him!

The road was much closer than he had expected it to be. It came out onto open ground and curved sharply to follow the edge of the woods.

Where the curve began, two ranks of drummers in tall bearskin helmets were beginning to swing toward him. Behind them, yellowy-brown ruts were hidden by a marching column. A mounted officer rode in the stubble field beside it.

Lex shrank back among the poplars. Here, right in front of him, the road was less than fifty yards away. At every wild beat of his heart, the head of that oncoming column was one quickstep closer.

But Lex wasn't looking at it. He was staring across half a mile of level fields toward the straight edge of another oak woods. The sky was a pale gray-blue above the tree-tops. Lower, close to the ground, there was another long, thin streak of almost the same color. He thought at first that he was seeing the sky beyond the dark trunks of the oaks.

Then he realized that there weren't any trees in front of that blue streak. They were all behind it!

He had found his own army!

The American militia was there, waiting, drawn up in long, solid battle lines.

But he had lost the race. In a minute, the British troops would be between him and those blue lines. The swaying

drums already were so close that he could see the drummers' hands moving, and their whirling sticks were
making a bright, yellow blur that glistened through the
yellow dust cloud drifting up around their striding legs.

Lex didn't stop to think. He jumped out into the
stubble field. In two steps, he was running.

The road flashed under him. He was past the head of
the British column. The broad farm fields stretched out
ahead. He ran with all his might.

Now the drums were behind him. They weren't so
loud. His muscles strained. His ears strained for the sound
of shouts, the slam of musket shots. He heard only the
crutshh . . . crutshh of his feet on brittle stubble and the
swishh . . . swishh of the dangling musket sling against his
leg. He looked back. The scarlet column was still marching down the road. All the soldiers were still in the ranks.
They weren't bothering to chase him.

He slowed down a little. His lungs ached and his ears
were ringing, but he was more than halfway to the blue
lines. He could see the round, black muzzles of iron
cannon in a row across the road. He could see the round,
bucket-shaped hats of the militia, like a row of thick posts
set on top of a wall. He could see a long, white streak of
faces watching him.

Suddenly a thin, shrill screech broke out. The gunners
crowded up between the guns. One of them waved his
arms and screeched again. And then it seemed to Lex that
all the men were yelling.

He looked back across his shoulder. The mounted
officer was coming after him, his horse at a dead gallop.
A long, straight saber flashed beside the horse's head.

Lex ran desperately, but, when he glanced back again,

he knew it was no use. The officer was going to ride him down.

He stopped. He turned around.

It wasn't till he raised the musket that he thought about his broken wrist. He couldn't aim the musket with one hand.

Lex dropped to one knee. He laid the heavy barrel across the other knee. His thumb jerked the lock back. His finger pulled the trigger. The lock clicked. That was all.

And that's all of me, Lex thought. The black horse was almost on him. It looked huge. It looked like a mountain getting ready to fall on him. No use to run. No use of anything. He stayed there, crouching on one knee.

The officer was shouting at him: "Drop that gun!"

Lex let the butt drop to the ground. The barrel leaned against his bent leg. His hand groped for the bayonet and dragged it from the scabbard.

This was what the tough old Continentals did when British cavalry had tried to ride them down. They knelt like this. They set their musket butts upon the ground and made an upward-slanting hedge of bayonets.

Lex twisted the hollow handle of the bayonet around the muzzle of the musket and heard the little click that locked it there. He jammed the iron-shod butt into the dirt. He gripped the stock and aimed the bayonet up toward the chest of the black horse.

The reins jerked. The horse swerved and went tearing by. The needle-sharp point of the bayonet caught on the rider's boot. The blade slid smoothly through the leather. Then it stuck. It dragged the officer out of the saddle.

The musket was torn from Lex's hand. The empty stirrup grazed his cheek. He threw himself backward, rolled, and felt the gunlock underneath his hip. When he came up on his knees, the musket lay there in the stubble, between him and the officer's slashed boot. The officer lay face down, stunned.

Lex snatched at the dusty barrel. He began to run again, with the butt bumping on the ground. The blue ranks were cheering when he reached the guns.

The gunners swarmed around him. Hard hands whacked him on the shoulders. He was hugged and hollered at and jostled. The shrill screech rose again above the clamor of excited voices. It sounded angry. It sounded like Joe Piery.

"Grits an' gravy!" The same puckered, leathery old face was there in front of him. The same scrawny hands were clawing at him. Lex was looking down at the dirty wrinkles on Joe Piery's bald head. "What you think you're doin'? Last time I seen you, you were runnin'. You been runnin' ever since, boy?"

"No," Lex gasped. The crazy question made him laugh, but he was panting so hard that the laugh was nothing but a giggle.

"Stop that!" Piery took him by the shirt and shook him. "Get ahold o' yourself, bub. Where'd you get that musket? An' the crossbelts? Where you been? Speak up!"

"With the British Fleet. They caught me. I got away." Lex had to stop for breath. "We killed Ross," he blurted.

"What's that?" The sharp words cut through Joe Piery's squeak and all the other startled voices. Horses came pushing into the circle of cannoneers around Lex.

An officer, with gold fringe on his shoulders and gold braid in rows across his chest, was frowning down at him. "Did you say you killed General Ross?"

"No, sir. Two boys shot him."

"How d' you know?"

"I saw them."

"Be careful. Don't lie to me." The officer had a big, red nose. The nose was peeling. His eyes were bright and hard. His face was so stern that he seemed to be glaring. "How do you know it was Ross?"

"You see here now, Gen'ral Stricker!" Joe Piery stepped up to him. "This here boy ain't lyin'! If he says he saw Ross killed, it's true. He'd know Gen'ral Ross anywheres. He'd ought to! Him an' me fought the whole British Army by ourselves in Washin'ton. There wasn't anybody else but us." Piery shook a skinny finger at the American general. "Your fine-feathered militia had all run away! Ross wasn't any farther from us than you can throw a hound-dog by the tail!" His voice rose to a screech again. "I mean a *big* hound-dog!"

"We'll find out," General Stricker said. He spoke to the commander of the battery. "Captain Montgomery, I'll have a word with the prisoner. Tell your men to bring him over here."

Lex turned his head and saw the officer who had tried to ride him down. Two gunners were half-leading and half-carrying him, with his arms across their shoulders. They came between two of the guns and halted.

"How long ago was General Ross killed?" The question cracked out like an order.

"An hour . . ." The British officer closed his mouth. His lips went white. Then his whole face turned fiery red.

The sharp question had caught him by surprise. He had been tricked into admitting that Ross was dead.

"Well, gentlemen," General Stricker looked at his staff clustered around him, "this news should make a difference. Captain Stevenson, please be so good as to inform the colonels. Ask them to tell their regiments. Send word back to the 6th; tell Colonel McDonald we shall try to stay here a little longer than we'd planned."

The captain turned his horse and raced away.

"You . . ." The general looked at Lex again, and he was no longer glaring. "What's your name, boy?"

Piery spoke up before Lex could answer.

"His name's Alexander Hamilton Landon, Gen'ral. His dad's Major Landon—the Virginia Brigade. Him an' me were in the same gun crew at Trenton. An' this here boy an' I had us another gun in Washin'ton. He'd come huntin' for his father, after Bladensburg. Hey!" Piery whirled around. "You ever find him, Lex? By gravy, I can see you didn't. He's all right, boy. He ain't seven miles from here right now."

Lex felt himself begin to shake. The relief was almost more than he could bear. He heard General Stricker saying, "Thank you, Landon." The voice seemed far away. Then it was loud again. "That boy's all tired out. Send him to the rear. Tell him how to find his father. Get him out of here."

Lex shook his head.

"If . . . if . . ." He stammered, and the woods seemed to be spinning. "I'd . . . I'd rather stay, if . . . if you please, sir."

The big, red, peeling nose was coming toward him. The general was bowing. His stern mouth was smiling.

"I hope all of us will feel that way, young Landon,"
Stricker said. He put a long, brass field glass to his eye
and peered across the fields beyond the guns. "Well,
gentlemen, by the look of things, we'll be having company
in about half an hour."

Lex thought that it was a queer way to talk about the
British Army.

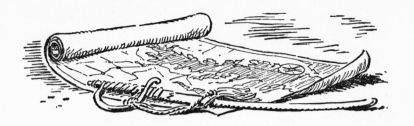

Chapter 11

"WE CAME HERE TO GET LICKED"

L ᴇx was lying in a shady place on the slope of a little knoll. It was a good place. He could look out underneath the branches of the trees and watch the army.

He felt safe for the first time in weeks. Maybe that was a strange way to feel, just before a battle, but the army was between him and the British. It was a good feeling.

He was cool, too. Joe Piery had poured cold water on his face and let him have a few swallows from the wooden canteen. Now the old man had disappeared. Lex hoped that he was filling the canteen. A bucket would be better. He could drink a bucketful of water, if Joe Piery'd let him.

"Wake up, boy." The rusty voice was just above him. "That's pretty good, hey, Doc? Whole British Army comin', but he goes to sleep. Lex, this here's Doc Martin. He's goin' to fix up that arm of yours."

Legs in stained white breeches knelt beside him. The stains looked like blood. A big, lumpy body leaned down. There were smears of blood, dark and sticky, on the pale-blue coat. The last time Lex had seen this man, he had been lifting the wounded sergeant and dumping him across the saddle of the bay horse and taking him away.

"Is he going to be all right?" Lex asked.

"Who?"

"That sergeant."

"He's hit right bad. Unconscious. Wasted my time on him, likely. So you're the boy that saw Ross killed, eh?"

"Yes, sir."

"I knew those lads that shot him. Dan Wells. Hank McComas. But I didn't know that it was Ross they shot." Dr. Martin snorted. "Crazy young fools! Greg Andre, too. It was Lieutenant Andre on the fence. They should have run. I wish we had more like them." He snorted again. "You're another crazy young fool! What did you think the Britishers would do to you, if they caught you with these crossbelts on you?"

"I guess I didn't think," Lex said.

"I guess you didn't. Piery, these belts are in my way. Help me get them off him."

In a few minutes, there were proper splints on Lex's wrist, with a clean bandage tight around it, and his arm was in a sling. The doctor tramped away.

"How you feel, son?" Piery asked.

"All right," Lex said. The wrist had been numb. It was burning again. "I feel fine."

"Time we were movin', then." The old man was

emptying the white cartridge box. "I'll just fetch these ca'tridges along." He stuffed them into the pockets of his ragged overalls, and picked up the musket. "This here's a long ways better than that popgun I borrowed off of you before. I lost that one. Hope you don't mind."

"I don't mind," Lex said.

"Truth is, I threw it away. It kind of slowed me down when I was runnin' through those backyards. I followed the army up to Baltimore, an' the Union Artillery let me join up with 'em. Yessir, Cap'n Montgomery knows a gunner when he sees one." Joe Piery sounded proud. He sounded like a rooster crowing. "No nonsense about me bein' too old. I'm actin' sergeant an' gun pointer. Yessir!"

They walked down the slope into the road. Wagons with white tops came jolting toward them, moving to the rear. Two-wheeled ammunition carts stood in the ditches. There were soldiers in the woods on both sides of the road. Most of them were sitting down or lying sprawled out on the ground.

"This here's our second line," Joe Piery said, "same as in the fight at Eutaw Springs, back in '81. September, it was, same as now."

"We lost that battle," Lex said.

"Same as now," Joe Piery said again. He sounded cheerful.

"You mean . . . ?"

"What you think I mean?" The old man was chuckling. "We came here to get licked."

"We didn't!"

"Use your wits, boy. We had Continentals, down to Eutaw Springs. The whole second line was Continentals. We ain't got nothin' but militia here. An' we ain't got

but three thousand of 'em. Hey . . ." He peered at Lex.
"You get a good look at the British Army?"

"Yes."

"How many men you think they've got?"

"Twice as many. Sailors, too; there must be a thousand
sailors. Cannon. More than we have. Bigger."

"Fine! That's fine!" Joe Piery didn't sound like a crowing rooster, now. He sounded like a pleased hen that had
laid an egg. "Yessir! That's just fine!"

"What's so fine about it?"

"Grits an' gravy! Can't you figure out nothin' for yourself? The more of 'em there are, the cockier they'll be, an'
the more we'll hurt 'em."

It didn't make much sense to Lex. He said so. That
made Piery mad.

"You settin' up to be a gen'ral, boy? It's you that ain't
got sense. Now see here, Lex—I'll lay it out for you, all
plain an' simple. We've got three thousand men. We can't
lick seven or eight thousand British reg'lars with three
thousand militia. Gen'ral Stricker knows it. Everybody
knows it."

"Then what's the use of fighting?"

"I told you!" Piery almost screeched. "To hurt 'em!
You stop arguin', Lex Landon. All you got to do is listen.
We've got five regiments, an' Gen'ral Stricker's formed
'em up in three lines. The first line's up ahead of us, at
the edge of the woods, with the guns in the middle an' a
regiment on each side of the road. The 5th Maryland is
on the right-hand side, an' the 27th's on the left. You
understand?"

"Yes, but . . ."

"Hold on till I'm finished, boy. We just came through

the second line. It's two more regiments. The 51st is three
hundred yards behind the 5th, an' the 39th is behind the
27th. You can't see the third line. It's half a mile back
down the road, behind a stream. The 6th Maryland is
there, with Bread-an'-Cheese Creek like a deep ditch in
front of it. Funny name for a creek, ain't it?"

Lex wasn't thinking about funny names. He was thinking about the army, scattered in three pieces.

"I see now why we're going to be whipped," he said.

"We're supposed to get licked!" Joe Piery really turned
his screech loose this time. "I keep tellin' you! We ain't
supposed to win! We're here to hurt 'em! Gen'ral Smith
an' Gen'ral Stricker don't want the British to come
swarmin' down on Baltimore, thinkin' they can whip the
whole United States. No, sir! They want to soften 'em up
first! They want to hurt the British Army so bad it'll think
twice before stormin' the Baltimore entrenchments."

"Then why don't we use all our men?"

"I s'pose you'd like to see the whole three thousand in
one line! You know what would happen? The Britishers
would smash us at one crack! But Stricker's goin' to make
'em take three cracks at us. An' that ain't all. He's tryin'
to make the Britishers come straight at us. We can hurt
'em bad if they do that. The first line will fight as long's
it can. It'll break, sure, but the British won't be lookin'
for no second line. We'll hurt 'em some more there. An'
when that line gives way, there's still the third line. The
army's goin' to stop runnin' when it gets to Bread-an'-
Cheese Creek. It's goin' to rally on the 6th, an' fight
again."

"But will it stop running?"

"I dunno," Piery said.

Chapter 12

THE BATTLE OF NORTH POINT

THE old man and the boy walked on along the shady road. It didn't seem possible, to Lex, that they were walking into battle.

The air was hot and still. The only sound was the buzz-zz-zzzz of a persistent deer fly, circling and darting around Piery's bald head. The old man kept slapping at it, but he didn't scold. He scuffed along with his thin shoulders hunched under the big musket, and his mouth puckered like an old leather purse with the drawstring pulled tight.

They came to a small opening in the woods. It was full of horses, stamping and hacking their heads up and down. Their trace chains rattled as they fought the flies. Soldiers holding to the bridles kept brushing the horses with leafy branches.

"Them's our gun teams," Piery said. "Remember

where they are, Lex. We'll want 'em pretty soon. An' when we do, we'll want 'em in a hurry."

The four-horse teams were still hitched to the limbers of the guns—the two low, chunky wheels and the bare axle where the ammunition chests were carried.

The ammunition chests were gone, now. Lex saw them in the road ahead, the small wooden boxes in a row behind the six small guns.

They had almost reached the guns when a harsh, whooping sound tore through the air. It was as if a giant had coughed suddenly, and then cleared his throat.

"What was that?" Joe Piery was staring at a thin line of smoke that curved above the treetops.

"Rockets!" Lex cried. He broke into a run.

"You heard 'em before?" The old man was jogging easily beside him. His eyes were bright with interest.

"Yes. I was . . . on a . . . rocket ship." His running feet pounded the words out of him in jerks. "There was . . . fight . . . on the Potomac."

"They're pretty bad, huh?"

"They're like . . ." Lex saw, in his mind, the blinding sheets of fire that leaped from the *Erebus*. He saw again the rockets plunging into the American battery, sticking in the red earth, flaming and exploding. "They're like . . . fence posts . . . burning."

"See anybody get killed by 'em?"

"No. I was too far . . ."

"Never mind how far away you were. Them rockets scared the daylights out of our militia, down to Bladensburg. You just tell the boys you didn't see nobody killed."

They came to the guns then, and Lex saw the British Army drawn up in battle order. Straight down the road, there was a solid mass of scarlet. To the right of it, the brigade of seamen was a bigger mass of dark blue. To the left, a long row of brass cannon glittered.

"See what I meant?" Joe Piery nudged his elbow. "They're goin' to come straight at us. That's a whole regiment in column of platoons, there on the road. Twenty men in each rank. Forty ranks deep, likely. Reg'lar batterin'-ram."

It looked to Lex as if half the British Army was getting ready to smash through the thin line of militia right here—at this very place where he was standing. The other half stretched out across the farm fields like a red-brick wall. The sun was blazing on it—on the thousands upon thousands of bright scarlet coats, with the sheen of bayonets above them like the hot gas that shines above a fiercely burning fire. The whole wall seemed to burn.

Less than an hour ago, Lex had been running for his life across those fields. It was hard to realize. The fields looked different somehow.

There was a white farmhouse that he hadn't noticed. There was an unpainted barn with a fenced-in stableyard around it. The buildings hid part of the British troops, but the battle line stretched far to the left beyond them. Haystacks dotted a mowed field between the farmhouse and the woods where the Americans were waiting.

A puff of smoke sprang up behind the stableyard. Then another . . . and another. Five. Six. The long, dark shapes of rockets leaped out of the smoke. Their hoarse whoop rose into a strangled screaming as they arched above the haystacks. The ranks of the militia wavered.

Most of the rockets plunged into the woods, but one of them came down in the mowed field. It quivered there a moment, its sharp, pointed nose half-buried in the earth. Lex saw a long stick like a stiff tail quivering above it.

Then it toppled over. It began to spit fire. It flopped. Its long tail beat the ground. Suddenly it jumped across the stubble, wriggling, sliding, spinning like a pinwheel. It left a trail of burning stubble in the field.

Lex heard Piery talking to the gunners:

"Them things ain't much." He sounded disappointed. "I'll tell you just how bad them rockets are. This boy here was a pris'ner on a British ship that used 'em. He was in a battle down on the Potomac. You know what he did when the first rocket let go, a few minutes back? He ran. Yessir! He ran *toward* the British! He ain't scared of rockets. He's seen 'em, an' he knows they ain't nothin' but a lot o' noise. You tell 'em, Lex. That's true, ain't it?"

"Yes," Lex said. It wasn't the whole truth, but he knew that the old man was trying to keep the cannoneers from getting nervous.

"No, sir," he heard Piery saying, "if a boy can stand them rockets, there ain't no call for us to worry. Cap'n Montgomery, we got a volunteer. He ain't got but one arm, but he can hold a linstock."

"We may need him, after a while." The captain gave him a tight grin. Then, as quietly as if he were sitting at a dinner table, asking someone to please pass the salt, he said, "Stand to your pieces, men. We'll see whether we can reach those people in the road."

The men jumped to their places. Joe Piery straddled the trail of the fourpounder that stood in the ditch. He squatted there, squinting along the black-iron barrel. His right hand clawed the air. The gun crew seized the wheels. The barrel turned a little.

"Easy," Piery said. "Easy. That's it." He scrambled up. The gunner standing in front of the axle, between the barrel and the left wheel, raised a linstock and blew on the match that smoldered at its tip.

"Number 1 piece . . ." Montgomery said. "Fire!"

The match came down on the touchhole. The four-pounder spouted black smoke and jumped backward. Lex felt as if his ears had been pushed together in the middle of his head.

"Number 2 . . . fire!" Montgomery was walking along the row of guns. "Number 3 . . . fire!"

Lex saw the smoke spread like a toadstool, and its underside was dirty-black and soft and poisonous-looking. His head rang like a kettle that was being beaten with a hammer. Faintly, he heard Piery squawking:

"Yessir! Straight at us, just the way we want 'em. Hurt 'em! Hurt 'em!"

But the mass of scarlet in the road did not seem to be hurt. It stood there, motionless and solid.

The British guns began to fire.

The first shells gouged dark furrows in the field in front of the blue infantry. They burst with bright-yellow flashes, with sharp, ripping crashes. The 27th shrank back from the fence. Then the men came back into a stiff, straight line. They stood staring at the shallow round holes blown into the earth by the explosions, and the raw dirt strewn around them.

The shells came and came. The yellow flashes seemed to walk along the fence from one end to the other. The militiamen stood with their shoulders humped and their heads pushed out as if they leaned against the fierce wind of a thunder-gust. But there had never been a thunder-gust like this! The shell bursts drove the smoke into their faces like gray rain.

Where the rocket had set fire to the field, there was a black, spreading circle of charred stubble with a rim of little flames around it. The flames had reached one of the haystacks. It was burning in long streaks of smoky red, and there was a brighter streak of red beyond it.

The streak moved steadily across the open ground at the far end of the field. Lex stared at it. The hot smoke of the guns was all around him, and his eyes were watering and smarting. He dug at them with his fists. He looked again, and this time he was sure. A column of British infantry was marching toward the woods beyond the 27th. And there were no Americans to stop it!

He reached out and got Joe Piery by the shoulder.

"Look!" he yelled. "They're not coming straight at us! They're flanking us! Look!" He pointed. "Over there . . . uhhh!"

The road blew up in front of him.

A red glare stood there like the side of a brick house. It was hard and hot. In a fraction of a second, Lex thought: I didn't know a color could be hard. But it was. It hit him in the eyes and face and on the chest and knocked him down. He didn't hear the rending crash of the shell that burst above the battery.

He lay on his back in the road and looked at the wheels of a gun. The wheels leaned toward each other. The gun had no barrel. He sat up, dizzy, and saw bodies in the road. One of them was only half a body.

Through the ringing in his head, Lex heard Captain Montgomery's voice, clear and steady:

"Number 1 . . . fire!"

He knew, then, that the wrecked gun hadn't been Joe Piery's.

But something was wrong with Number 1. There weren't as many men around it as there should be. And Piery shouldn't have the linstock in his hand. It was dangerous to stand behind the gun and lay the lighted match upon the priming. The recoil would hurl the gun against Piery. It could break his legs against the axle, or a wheel could crush him.

The fourpounder said "Buhh!" Joe Piery jumped. The wheel rolled past him, but the iron rim struck his chin. As he fell, the hub caught his knee and threw him clear. He dropped the linstock, and the wheel rolled over it and broke it. The wooden shaft snapped like a bone.

Lex heard the snap. It seemed impossible to hear so small a noise, but there it was. In the sudden pause between kkr-ramm-kr-rr-annk of shell bursts and the bluhh-ughh of the guns, the only sounds were the far-off whooping of more rockets and the drumming hoofbeats of a horse, behind him in the lane.

The horse slid to a stop. A voice bawled above him: "Montgomery! Montgomery, we're being flanked! Stricker's sending in the second line. He says send two guns! He says send them quick!"

Captain Montgomery said, "Thank you, Major Frailey. Right away." He turned toward the guns. "Lieutenant Stiles, will you please . . . ?"

Two gun teams came trotting. The limbers swung around. They went away again, with two guns clattering behind them, and vanished in the woods. The three small cannon in the road looked lonely after they were gone.

Joe Piery was sitting up. Blood trickled from his chin.

He had the slivered linstock in his hand. He brandished it at Lex.

"Git up! Grab ahold of this thing! I got three men down. Move, will you? You're second-gunner. Git this linstock lighted!"

Then Lex was standing in the second-gunner's place, between the barrel and the left wheel. The broken linstock leaned against the axle. Piery threw a small, gray bundle at him. He caught the flannel powder bag with his bent arm, slid the bag into the barrel, and the first gunner rammed it down. Another bundle hit him in the ribs. It was hard and heavy—musket balls sewed into stiff, coarse cloth. He felt the hot mouth of the cannon burn his hand as he pushed the grapeshot in.

"Fire!" The captain's calm voice steadied him. He seized the linstock and blew on the match, until the tip was a clean red glow. The priming powder hissed. The touchhole spurted white smoke. The gun jumped and ran backward.

And then a shell burst in the faces of the militia on the bank above him. It blew one man out of the line. He slid slowly down the bank, headfirst into the ditch.

He's dead, Lex thought, but there was no time to make sure. There was no time to think. There was no time to be afraid. Lex knew what he must do.

He hooked his arm around a wheel spoke, and saw Captain Montgomery heaving at the other wheel. They rolled the gun back into place.

Through the thinning smoke, Lex saw the fields again. Two more haystacks were on fire. Beyond them, the white farmhouse and the barn were burning.

The two guns that had disappeared into the woods were

trying to knock out the rocket battery behind the stableyard. They had set fire to the buildings, but they hadn't
smashed the battery. The rockets soared above the leaping
flames like dark flights of enormous whooping cranes.

The British battle line began to move.

"All guns!" Montgomery shouted. "Load with canister!"

Joe Piery took a shiny can from the ammunition chest.
It rattled as Lex caught it. He knew that it was filled with
musket balls and broken pieces of old scrap iron. But it
would take more than the cans to stop that solid mass of
redcoats coming down the road.

"Prime! Take aim! Fire!"

Lex saw a sudden swirl in the mass of scarlet. He saw
men go down, and other men staggering into the field
before they fell.

"We hurt 'em!" Piery cried.

But the British ranks closed up. The human battering-
ram came on.

The three guns fired and fired.

They couldn't stop the British battle line. It came like
a brick wall, moving. It knocked down the farmyard
fences. It was in the mowed field, now. The thick column
in the road was halfway to the guns, and the thousand
seamen were coming like a blue wave rolling in from
the Atlantic.

Lex was panting. Sweat streamed down his face. His
arm ached from catching the cans as Piery tossed them.
His hand was blistered by the hot iron of the cannon
muzzle.

He saw the British only in quick glimpses. A second-
gunner had to keep his back turned toward the enemy.

He wasn't afraid—yet. There was too much to do. Slide the powder bag into the barrel. Push the can after it. Snatch the linstock. Blow the match. Fire! But knowing that the British were behind him, coming nearer every second, gave him a queer feeling. It made his back feel cold.

Lex was heaving at the wheel again when a foaming horse burst from the woods. The rider shouted at Montgomery:

"The 51st has broken! Half the 39th, too! They're running! Stricker says, 'Hold on as long's you can. Hold on to the last thin minute! But get the guns away!' "

Montgomery looked at his three guns. He looked at the bodies in the road, and at the wounded men who lay propped up against the bank.

"We may not have enough men left," he said.

The British infantry came through the smoke between the burning haystacks.

An American officer came walking along the edge of the field, along the fence in front of the 27th. A flag hung limply from a slim pole in his hands. The flag was too long for the pole. Its red-and-white stripes hung down over his face. He kept brushing them aside. When he came to the last post of the fence, he used the rails for steps. He climbed up and braced one leg against the post. His voice rang out:

"Attention!" The feathers in the bucket-shaped caps fluttered. The ranks stiffened. "In a minute, now, we're going to fire. Not all at once. Platoon volleys, starting at the right. The 5th will fire first. Remember—don't shoot until I tell you. One volley! After that, keep firing as fast as you can load."

He swung the flag. The long stripes swooped out above the road and over the gun standing in the ditch. Lex saw a circle of white stars against the blue. It wasn't a new flag. The clear voice rang again:

"You know where this flag's been! My father carried it at Cowpens, in the Revolution. Sergeant Bill Batchelor— the old 3rd Maryland—the old Continentals! We whipped the British that day! They got my father, but they didn't get this flag! *And they're not going to get it!* We . . ."

The first American volley crashed out like a cannon shot.

"There we go!" The white stars dipped and swung. The stripes blew straight. "It's starting, boys! You know what we've got to do. We're going to hang on until the Britishers are fifteen feet away. That's not so close! That's five whole yards! The British bayonets aren't five yards long. They just look as if they were."

The second volley slammed.

"Just forget about their bayonets. We aren't going to wait for them. But we're not leaving yet!" Ensign Batchelor's face was whiter than the swooping stars, but he was grinning at the men below him. "You wait for me, I'll wait for you. Just stay right here as long as you can see this flag!"

The lightning crashes of the volleys were coming closer. They were louder than the guns, now. In the short silences between them, Lex still heard the ensign talking:

"It's almost our turn, boys. Remember . . . aim low! Don't aim at the buckles on the crossbelts. Aim *below* them. *Ready . . . !*"

The 5th Maryland's last volley and the first volley of the 27th blazed almost together. The air shook, and Lex felt his body shaking. I'm not scared! I'm not! And he wasn't—not the way he had been. But he was trembling with exhaustion.

He almost dropped the powder bag that hit him in the ribs. He juggled it, hugged it to his stomach, and ran to the muzzle of the gun. The dripping sponge was just sliding in. The hot iron hissed and steamed. On the bank above him, the militia began to yell:

"Yiaa-a-ahh! Yeeaa-aaa-aaahhh! They've stopped! Look a' that! By glory, we stopped 'em!"

The gray-flannel cartridge bumped on the steaming muzzle. Lex shoved it in. He turned to look.

His breath caught in his throat. He tried to swallow. He couldn't.

He hadn't realized the British were so close!

They were so close he could see the sweating faces in the front rank of the battering-ram in the road. He could see the ridges of the men's fingers, gripping the musket stocks.

The British battle line stood less than a hundred yards from the fence and the three little guns!

There were bodies in the field behind it. There were other bodies in the road, and there were wounded men scrabbling and crawling through the scorched stubble. But the scarlet ranks were closed up. They still looked as solid as a brick wall.

"Yiaa-aahh!" The cheering was fainter, now. The Americans were beginning to realize that they hadn't stopped the enemy. There were only two regiments and part of another one left in their front line. There was no second line at all. There were fewer than fourteen hundred militia behind the fence. They were facing more

than four thousand veteran regulars. All along the half
mile of the British front, they could see the officers standing with their backs turned as if to show their contempt.
They could hear the officers giving orders—the quick,
crisp words of command. The yells changed to a kind of
wailing:

"Look out! They're going to shoot! Aahh . . . Look
out!"

The whole British battle line seemed to explode.

A level sheet of fire leaped from the thousands of
muskets.

The crash shook the earth. Lex felt it through his shoes.

A cloud of flame-lighted smoke rolled toward the
American line.

The line wasn't a line any more. It was broken and
sagging. It was groups of men huddling together, and
men shrinking back from the fence and hiding behind the
trees, and men clutching the top rail and putting their
heads on the rail and being sick, and other men holding
their muskets as if they were clubs or fish poles or canes
and they had forgotten what muskets were for.

The British Army came out through the rolling smoke.

It came in pieces, but they were not broken pieces.
Each one was half a battalion in three steady ranks. They
ran forward fifteen paces. They halted and fired. The
other halves of the battalions came on a run through the
smoke, and filled up the gaps between them, and halted,
and fired.

This was the terrible British attack that had smashed
Napoleon's finest troops. This was the last maneuver
before the bayonet charge.

Raw militia could not stand up to soldiers like these.

Fourteen hundred men couldn't possibly fight four thousand.

But the raw militiamen were standing up. They were coming back to the fence. They laid their musket barrels on the top rail and fired at the level red flashes that came through the boiling smoke and at the red coats that loomed through the smoke.

The old Cowpens flag was swinging in long, slow swoops. The stripes swung out over Lex's head as Joe Piery put another can in his hand. The old man wasn't tossing the canister charges now; the smoke was too thick to see them. The smooth metal felt cool. It felt good on his blistered hand.

The musket roar was like thunder now—like thunder that never stopped. It blotted out the crack of the little gun; it soaked up the sound like a sponge.

The fourpounder jumped and slid backward. Lex leaped for the wheel. The captain was already there. His hand gripped Lex's sleeve and pulled him close.

"You know where the gun teams are." Montgomery's mouth was against Lex's ear. "Go get them! *Run!*"

He ran. He passed a soldier who limped, with his musket tucked under his arm like a crutch. He caught a glimpse of a gray-haired militiaman leaning against a tree, his hands over his eyes and blood running between his fingers. He had a glimpse of two other men leaning against each other, holding each other up as they hobbled along the road.

Lex came to the clearing where the gun limbers waited. He screamed at the nearest man, choked from the sting of the powder fumes in his throat, tried to scream again, and pointed in the direction of the guns. The man understood. He yelled at the other horse holders, and then he was yelling at Lex:

"Get up there!" He slapped the short reins into Lex's hand. "Get on this horse!" He let go of the bridle. He seized Lex by the belt, behind, and put the other hand on the seat of his pants and heaved. He fairly threw Lex onto the back of the plunging lead horse. His arm swung, and his hand came down with a stinging slap on the horse's flank.

And then the team was tearing along the road, with the limber bouncing and swaying behind it, and Lex was clinging desperately with his one hand and his legs.

He was slipping. He couldn't hold on. *But he had to hold on!* The guns were just ahead now. They were dim in the smoke, and the few remaining gunners were like dim ghosts in the twilight of smoke. The horses were galloping wildly. He couldn't control them. *He had to!* He couldn't turn them. *He had to!* And somehow he did.

The horses leaned as they turned. The limber swerved into the ditch. The wheels flung a shower of dirt over three men who stooped by the trail of a gun.

The men lifted the trail. They slid its iron ring over the hook on the limber.

Lex held the reins taut. He tried to hold the team steady. He twisted his head around, watching the gunners, waiting for them to leap onto the horses' backs—but they didn't. They stepped aside, out of the way of the wheels. Their arms waved. They made frantic motions for him to go.

He saw that one of them was Captain Montgomery. The captain was drawing his sword.

He saw Joe Piery ramming another charge into

Number 1 gun. He looked up at the fence and the men who had been there were gone and the flag was gone.

The gun fired its last shot. It blew a puffball of smoke into the faces of British soldiers with wide-open, yelling mouths and bayonets slanting before them.

Captain Montgomery was running toward Lex. His sword gleamed in his hand. He beat at the snorting team with the flat of the blade. The horses lunged.

The last thing Lex saw of the battle was Joe Piery's back. The old man stood with his back to the gun and the long wooden rammer clutched in his scrawny hands as the bayonets came.

Chapter 13

WHEN FREE MEN SHALL STAND

THE history books seldom mention the battle in which Lex Landon and Joe Piery fought.

When they do, they say the American Army ran away. They say it was panic-stricken. They say it turned into a terrified mob.

That is partly true, but it isn't all of the truth. The broken militia regiments fled through the woods. That is true. They didn't look much like an army; they looked a good deal like a panicky mob. That also is true. An army running away from an enemy three times as strong is quite likely to look like a mob.

But the books don't say the American soldiers were *ordered* to run. They don't say the retreat was planned, a long time before the battle, because General Stricker and General Smith—the commander in chief at Baltimore —wanted to save their men to fight the British again.

They don't tell what happened after the front line broke and the soldiers began to run.

They ran half a mile, and stopped! It was hard to believe, but Lex Landon saw it happen.

His gun team was still at full gallop when it broke out of the woods with the cannon lurching behind it. The road crossed a grassy meadow and came to a shallow ravine and a creek and a plank bridge over the creek. The flying hoofs drummed on the bridge. The wheels made a hollow thunder on the loose planks.

And there, on the opposite bank, was another blue battle line!

The 6th Maryland Infantry stood where Joe Piery had said it would be. It stood in three ranks, knee-deep in the ripened grass, and the ranks were rigid and straight. They hadn't been shaken at all by the sight of the fleeing men who poured from the woods, and swarmed helter-skelter across the meadow, and floundered down into the creek.

Then there were hands at the bridles, slowing the team, and Lex was sliding off. He was falling. It didn't matter. He'd brought the gun back.

He lay in the grass and watched the wheels going away from him, up the slope, and the tilted barrel dragging its nose in the dust behind.

The wheels stopped. The black muzzle came up. The barrel turned into three. Lex shook his head. He was dizzy, but not that dizzy! He looked again, and there were really three cannon, hub to hub in the road, and Lieutenant Stiles was wiping a dusty barrel with a white handkerchief. The lieutenant had brought back both of his guns!

The planks rumbled again. Another four-horse team

trotted over the bridge, with four gunners astride. Montgomery swung himself down from the wheel horse. Stiles came to meet him.

"Captain! Thank God! I'm glad to see you."

"I'm glad to be here." Montgomery's face was yellow with powder stains and the dust that his sweat had turned into mud. "Let me borrow that handkerchief, will you?" He scrubbed at his face with the dirty cloth. "We lost Number 1 gun. The men tried to save it. John Lamb. Jim Davidson. Two or three others. They tried to fight the whole army! That crazy old fellow . . . What was his name?"

"Leary," Stiles said. "Something like that."

Lex felt a rush of anger. It lifted him to his feet.

"He wasn't crazy! He wasn't! You don't even know his name! Now . . ." His voice quavered. It turned to a croak. "Now he's dead."

"No," Captain Montgomery said. "He's not dead. They knocked him down once. He got up again. The rammer broke. I saw them holding him. He's a prisoner, but he's alive. Very much alive. He was kicking their shins."

"Oh," Lex said weakly, and felt the tears hot in his eyes.

"Here. . . ." The captain held out the soiled handkerchief. Then he pulled it back quickly and wadded it in his hand. Lex let on that he hadn't noticed. "You saved the gun, Landon. Good man." Not good boy, but good *man*. Lex forgave him for not remembering Joe Piery's name.

They walked up the slope. Lex unhooked the wooden sponge bucket that hung from the axle. He walked down to the creek and waded out, upstream from the hurrying soldiers whose feet were churning the clear water into muck. He carried the bucket back to the gun. While he sponged out the barrel, he watched the militia coming up out of the creek.

They came like a crowd of scarecrows. Their faces were filthy with sweat-caked dirt. Their mouths were black smears from tearing the paper musket cartridges with their teeth. The bright, sky-colored jackets were black with their sweat, and their breeches were crisscrossed with bramble rips and streaked with the powdery, red-brown dust of dead leaves. They walked like old men.

But they still had their muskets. They stopped when they came to the motionless ranks of the 6th. They had enough spirit left to raise a cheer for the half-platoon of the 27th that marched smartly over the bridge behind the old Cowpens flag.

"Fall in!" shouted the officers. "Over here, Baltimore Yeagers! Washington Blues . . . Mechanical Volunteers . . . !" The names of the companies rang. "Independents . . . ! Jefferson Blues on the left! Fall in, men! Fall in!"

The militia obeyed. They formed ranks on both sides of the 6th. The men who had run away stood in line of battle, ready to fight again.

General Stricker rode slowly along the line. There was a high, proud look about him. In front of each regiment, he stopped and lifted his hat. When he came to the Union Artillery, he bowed and said, "Thank you, gentlemen." He held his hat in his hand while he talked to Captain Montgomery.

"We've seen something today, John," he said.

"Yes, sir," Montgomery answered. "It's been like a miracle."

"It has been a miracle, John. I hoped we'd be able to rally, but . . . Well, the Maryland Continentals broke at Hobkirk's Hill; they ran, and they didn't come back. Asking militia to run, and then stop and re-form, was asking more than I had any right to expect. Look at these men!"

Stricker lifted himself in the saddle. He stood in the stirrups, and his eyes traveled along the front of the shabby, tired, dirty regiments.

"They're worth looking at." His big, peeling nose had taken another bad sunscald. It glowed like a red-hot coal in his face. "Only one regiment ever in battle before— and routed that time. It takes *men* to come back and stand up for another licking." Stricker's whole face seemed to glow with his pride. "All the miracles aren't in the Bible. Men don't realize what they can do, till they stand with their homes at their backs and an enemy coming to burn them."

"Yes, sir," Montgomery said. Stricker looked at him sharply.

"What's the matter, John?"

"We're short on ammunition."

"How short?"

"Only five rounds of canister left. Plenty of round shot, but it will take more than a miracle to stop them with solid shot."

"I've sent back for the ammunition wagons," Stricker said. "The bread wagons, too. We ought to get the men fed. I've always thought we wiped out the British at Cowpens because Tarleton piled his troops into action hungry." He pulled out his watch. "Five and a half o'clock. I wonder what's keeping our friends. They should at least have their skirmishers on us, by now. They would have, likely, if Ross hadn't been killed. Well . . . if they want more time, they can have it."

"How much time?" Montgomery asked.

"We'll stay here till sundown. Tell your men to rest. The infantry will have to eat standing up; I'm going to hold them in ranks. But let your men lie down while they can. They've had harder work than the rest of us."

Stricker bowed again to the men at the guns, and rode on along the line.

The army waited, and watched for the first red flicker of British skirmishers at the edge of the woods. The gunners sprawled in the little patches of shade beside the limbers or under the guns. Some of them slept, but Lex was too restless to rest. He kept fussing around the cannon that he had brought back, wiping the barrel, pricking the flakes of burned powder out of the touchhole.

He was still at it when the wagons pulled up, and then there were cans to carry and stow in the ammunition chests, and armloads of gray-flannel cartridges.

"How long since you've eaten, Landon?"

He looked up and saw Captain Montgomery with half a loaf of bread in each hand and a whole loaf tucked under each arm.

"I . . . I'm not sure." Lex tried to remember. The last food he could think of was the brined-beef stew Mr. Key had brought him on board the *Surprise*. "I guess it was two days ago."

"Good grief! Here . . . grab one of these loaves. Fresh-baked this morning. That's one advantage of having a war close to home. About the only advantage. Now stop fidgeting over that gun. I don't want you worn-out when we

need you. I don't want that gun worn-out, either."
Montgomery thumped his boot heel against the hard
ground. "Not much of a bed. Go find a soft place, if you
can, and lie down. Don't worry about the redcoats. You'll
know when they get here, all right."

Lex wandered away. He found an uprooted pine, with
a weedy hole where the roots had been. When he stamped
down the weeds, they didn't make a bad bed. The sun was
low; the butt of the pine threw a shadow into the hole.
He leaned back and started to work on the bread.

After the first bite, he was ravenous. His empty stomach
came to life. It seemed to be climbing up into his chest
to get the bread quickly.

But a great wave of tiredness was climbing up through
him also. He hadn't slept since the afternoon Frank Key
had fed him. He opened his mouth for another bite, and
yawned, and the yawn was too big for the bite. The loaf
slipped out of his hand.

Chapter 14

THE ATTACK ON FORT McHENRY

Lᴇx shivered in his sleep. The shiver was part of his dream. He was trying once more to escape from the British frigate.

Even in the dream, he knew he had tried it before. He knew he'd been clumsy about it. He'd been as awkward as his sister, trying to dive from the rail of the *Lex and Robin,* and doing belly-whoppers instead. He had broken his arm, and they'd caught him.

This time he was being more careful. He was doing everything right. He had made a clean dive from the bulwark of the *Surprise,* and he had hit the water head-first, with no splash at all. He shivered because the river was colder than he had expected, after the baking heat of the deck.

And then something went wrong with the dream.

Something that felt like seaweed was dragging across his face, and his hand was scrabbling in mud. His dive must have taken him all the way to the bottom, and he must have hit something again, with his arm. The same arm. It burned all the way to his shoulder.

The next shiver woke him up. Even then, he had a feeling that he was under water. He was soaking wet. His hair was plastered down over his forehead. There *were* wet weeds against his face, and his hand *was* dabbling in greasy mud.

He was lying in the hole where the roots of the pine tree had been and the hole was a third full of water and his hand and one leg lay in the muddy pool. He had rolled in his sleep, and his broken wrist was cramped underneath his hipbone. It hurt like toothache. Now that he was awake, he could feel the pain throbbing all the way up through his neck and into his jaw.

He rolled over on his back and looked up into a slow, gray drizzle that leaked from a sky he couldn't see. It must be an hour after sunset, to be so dark.

Sunset! General Stricker had told Montgomery that the army would wait for the British until the sun went down! Lex didn't take time to get up. He walked on his knees through the puddle and peered out over the wet, crumbly rim of the hole.

The army was gone!

It couldn't be gone. It had to be here! It had to! Maybe it had only moved down the slope of the meadow. Maybe the army was using the creek itself as a trench.

He pulled himself up and ran through the sopping grass. The slope was empty. So was the ravine. Even the bridge was gone. The planks had been taken up, and the timbers that held them had been hacked through with axes and tumbled into the water. The planks had been piled up and burned. The smell was bitter and sharp in the drizzle.

Lex stood and stared at the ruined bridge and suddenly realized that he could see it more plainly. He could see the separate splinters fuzzing out from the broken ends of the timbers. He could even see little chips in the trampled mud. This wasn't evening! It wasn't an hour after sunset. It was an hour after dawn! He had slept while the guns rumbled by, and two thousand men went tramping away down the road.

Lex shivered again. He had slept all night with nothing between him and the enemy!

Something moved at the edge of the woods. A man stepped out into the meadow, another came out beside him. Their coats weren't red. They looked black because they were soaked with rain.

Lex threw himself flat, but the British patrol had already seen him. The two men began to run toward him. Behind them, a skirmish line trotted out of the woods. Lex sprang to his feet. Shots thumped in the sodden air. The skirmishers whooped.

And then he was running, with the British hunting cry shrill in his ears: "Tallyho-o-ooo!"

He didn't want to be hunted. He couldn't stand it again. He sobbed as he ran.

Long after the British skirmishers had given up the chase, it was the sound of his own blubbering that brought him to his senses. He snuffled, started to wipe his nose on his sleeve, and suddenly thought of General Stricker's raw, half-skinned nose. How would Stricker have looked, riding along the battle line, lifting his hat to the men in the ranks, and then using his sleeve? Lex dropped his arm quickly, as if the whole army could see, and used a handful of grass to attend to his nose.

The drizzle had stopped. Full daylight was coming fast. It was pale, washed-out daylight, as if the rain had faded it somehow. He could see a long way, over low humpy ridges and rolling fields, and there were no houses in sight, but somewhere he heard a door slam.

That hard, jarring sound was familiar. He'd heard it before. He had stood on the drill field back home, in a crooked line of boys and old men, and strained his ears for the sound to repeat itself. Captain Cutcheon had shouted, "Mortars! The Britishers are using mortars on Fort Washington."

Now the British Fleet must be using those huge sea mortars to smash Fort McHenry in Baltimore Harbor.

The next gentle ridge dropped into a shallow valley with a little stream like a silver thread running through it. He followed the stream toward the sound that grew louder and louder.

The familiar, sour smell of tide flats prickled his nose. Far in the distance, he saw the white top of a lighthouse. The stream dropped abruptly over a shelf of yellowish stone. Lex jumped from the ledge into smooth, black mud, and the shock of three mortars firing at once jarred his body as if his feet had struck solid rock instead of soft muck. He went floundering through the tide swamp toward a dirty-brown sheet of water that stretched away for two miles to another low, swampy shore.

He could not see the fort. It must be hidden behind

the bluff where the lighthouse stood, a mile or more up the river.

But out in midstream, less than a mile down the Patapsco, the British warships lay in two curving lines. Their sails were furled. Their mastheads stuck up through a straw-colored, motionless bank of smoke that lay on their upper spars like a thatch roof laid upon rafters.

He knew those ships!

There were six in the nearest line. How well he knew some of them!

That was *Erebus* there, at the end of the arc, anchored broadside across the current. The rest were the ships with the terrible names—*Terror* and *Meteor, Aetna, Volcano,* and *Devastation.* They lay with their long, level bowsprits pointed upstream. He could see the dark lumps of the mortars that crouched on their decks.

A fountain of smoke spouted up from one of the bomb ships. A black speck jumped out of the smoke. It seemed to be going straight up to the sky.

Then another dark gush . . . and another . . . another . . . another. Five black specks now. Five of those monstrous iron shells, climbing the sky at once. It was like watching a juggler keeping five balls in the air at one time.

They seemed to go on forever. Lex lost them in a shimmering layer of haze. And then, far above it, he saw them against the white clouds.

The first one turned slowly. So slowly! It seemed to be stuck to the clouds.

One after another, the bombs made those lazy turns

and began to fall. They rolled down the sky like balls
rolling down a steep roof . . . faster . . . and faster . . . until
they plunged out of sight behind the bluff.

All Lex saw when they burst was the quick, pale flash
and a quick, red glow on the white wall of the lighthouse.
Flash . . . flash . . . and two flashes together . . . and the
winking red glow.

While the explosions still crackled, the *Erebus* fired. A
steep-slanting wall of smoke leaned out from her side. A
torrent of fire and sparks poured down from twenty
rockets set off in a single volley. For a moment, the torrent
hung like a burning Niagara over the flame-lighted river
. . . and slowly collapsed . . . and sank into the water in a
dark rain of ashes.

The long cylinder shapes of the rockets soared up in
an even row—as if, Lex thought, the log wall of a stock-
aded fort had been struck by a hurricane and was being
carried up into the sky. The rockets climbed faster than
the bombs of the mortar ships, but not quite so steeply—
not nearly so high. At a thousand feet, they arched down
and dived toward the hidden fort.

Faint, far away, Lex heard the thudding of cannon. He
looked again at the ships—the four bigger ships in the
second line. They were frigates, but they were not firing.
That dull, distant thudding must come from the guns in
the fort.

But there were no splashes of shot in the water around
the fleet. He watched for them until the brown ripples
began to blur, and he looked away to rest his eyes for a
moment.

He saw them, then, three tiny flecks of white spray
that were gone so quickly he wasn't sure they had been

there. They couldn't have been there! They certainly shouldn't have been—half a mile from the nearest ship. But they came again, four scattered splashes this time, and all of them half a mile short. No wonder Frank Key didn't think much of Fort McHenry. If it couldn't do better than that . . .

It couldn't. Its guns were outranged. They ceased firing. The five mortar ships and the rocket cruiser pounded and pounded away at the fort that couldn't hit back.

Lex felt his heart sink. He thought of Fort Washington, blown up by its own defenders because they could not endure the terrible mortar shells. Was the same thing going to happen again?

He scrambled up to the top of the riverbank and began to run. He had to know what was happening to that silent and helpless fort.

Chapter 15

A STICK OF STRIPED PEPPERMINT CANDY

FORT MCHENRY was a volcano, erupting. It thundered and flamed. A black pillar of smoke towered up from its fiery crater.

The smoke twisted and writhed. It spread out at the top of the pillar. It thickened and swelled and spread like an ugly, dark cloud that built itself slowly higher and higher into the sky.

Blinding flashes came out of the cloud. They drove the smoke downward upon the brick walls and the roofs of the barracks that stood like the rim of a crater around the parade ground. The seething masses of smoke boiled over the barracks roofs and flowed down the walls of the fort like sheets of black, bubbling lava.

Every minute, a mortar shell dropped from the sky,

and the fort erupted again with a shuddering crash and a red glare that broke into darting splinters of flame.

Every minute, the rockets came darting. They stuck in the earth and stood upright in circles of furious fire that burst from their burning warheads.

On the opposite shore of the channel that led to Baltimore's inner harbor, Lex Landon watched, and wondered how men could live in that blazing, exploding inferno.

The stunning concussions had driven him back from the edge of the bluff. He leaned now with his shoulders set to the wall of the lighthouse, and felt the wall quiver against his flesh. Even here, with the channel between him and the fort, the blasts of the shells came as solid pushes against his chest. And the clang of the bursting iron made his eardrums ring, and the scream of the flying fragments was like the wild screaming of horses trapped in a burning barn.

But there were men in McHenry, and somehow they were still alive. He could see them crouching behind the low, brick-and-sod parapet outside the fort, and lying flat on the timber platform of a mud-walled battery close to the water's edge. When the bombs ripped the smoke cloud apart, he could see other men in the embrasures of the nearest brick bastion, under a drooping flag.

It was an enormous flag. Sometimes the gusts of three or four mortar shells, bursting together, stirred and lifted the stripes, and the stars came out for a moment. But most of the time the flag hung limp. It clung to its staff like a stick of striped peppermint candy.

Lex would have liked to be up on the iron-railed walkway that circled the lighthouse, high over his head. From up there, he thought, he could probably look across the crests of the ridges, toward Baltimore, and see the entrenchments Joe Piery had talked about. That was where the army must be.

But the walkway was some kind of signal station, and men in naval uniforms were watching the British Fleet with telescopes. They wouldn't welcome him, likely.

"Where's your post?" The question boomed in his ear and jerked him away from the wall.

A man in a short seaman's jacket stood at the top of a path that zigzagged up from the beach. An iron pot hung from the crook of his elbow. Buckets were strung by their handles along his other arm. He didn't look like an officer, but his voice was hard with authority.

"I'll have no straggling." His face was hard with suspicion. "Is that sling a fake?"

Lex set his jaw. He had a resentful answer on the tip of his tongue, but the buckets were steaming. The unbelievable smells of fried ham and coffee were in his nose, and his tongue was swimming. He had to swallow twice before he could get out a "No."

"What's wrong with your arm?"

"It's broken."

"It had better be. We'll find out. Where've you been, to get hurt?"

"The *Surprise*. I . . ."

"Deserter, uh?"

"No!"

"That's a new dodge—denying it. You're either deserter or spy. We've had a few spies, and mostly they claim they're deserters."

"I'm not a spy!"

"You'll have to prove it, my lad."

Both Lex's tongue and his stomach forgot about coffee and ham. His stomach was sick with this brutal unfairness, and his tongue was sharp with his anger:

"I don't have to prove it to *you!* I'm not in your helpless navy. I'm in the army. I'm in the Union Artillery. *We* didn't have to stop firing yesterday because our guns couldn't shoot far enough! We . . ."

"Back your topsails, young fellow." Suspicion was turning to doubt in the sailor's face. "Say that again. Were you in that fight at North Point?"

"I was there. I don't know what it's called."

"Who's in command of the Union Artillery?"

"Captain Montgomery."

"Who's next in command?"

"Lieutenant Stiles. If that's not enough, the 5th Maryland and the 27th were in the first line. The 39th, after the British started to flank us. The 6th . . ."

"What's this chat about General Ross?"

"He was killed."

"So . . . You saw it, eh? Might as well go the whole hog with this yarn."

"Yes! I saw it!"

"Hmmm." The sailor swayed backward and boomed up at the men on the walkway: "Captain Rutter! Here's a fellow says he saw Ross get killed."

"He did?" A fore-and-aft hat leaned over the rail. "Bring him up, Wynn."

"Wynn Herman—that's me." The buckets spilled coffee over their rims as he pushed out his hand. "Captain, privateer *Mary Oursler*. She's lying back of the barricade. Rutter's captain of the gun-barge flotilla. What's your name? Landon, uh? Give us the whole yarn,

Landon. All we know about that North Point battle is that there was a battle."

An hour later, Lex had finished the story and also a bucket of coffee and more than his share of fried ham. He was on the walkway with Captain Rutter's telescope at his eye, and the powerful glass was bringing the army so close that he felt he need only call out and the men in the lines would hear him.

His father might hear him!

Lex had an almost irresistible impulse to shout, "Major Landon! Major Tom Landon!"

It was silly and childish, likely, to think he could find one face among thousands of faces, a mile and a half away. Nevertheless, he began to search along the trenches that scarred the bare slopes of those distant hills.

And then he was shivering as he had shivered, a few hours ago, in his dream.

He had a good reason this time. He was seeing a miracle, just as John Stricker had seen one. A cold chill of amazed delight and excitement, and a pride like General Stricker's, was running through his whole body. As the glass traveled slowly along the hills, massive fieldworks seemed to jump toward him—redoubts that looked as solid as forts—redans—rifle pits—walls made of tree trunks with ax-sharpened tops—and entanglements made of whole trees with the tips of their branches cut to sharp points, waiting to trap the British infantry if they tried to attack. And cannon! Field guns standing hub to hub in long rows. Guns from the new warships still not quite ready for sea, on ponderous mountings of timber.

The American fieldworks lay on the hills in an enormous horseshoe, facing the roads and the fields by which the British Army must come. Lex counted 125 cannon, and there were still more to be counted.

The miracle that had been wrought on those hills had been wrought in less than three weeks, since the burning of Washington. It had been wrought by men who weren't soldiers, but only everyday men with their country and homes to protect.

For the first time in his life, Lex Landon had a sense of the power of this young, raw country of his—of the strength never yet really used.

The shiver was at his lips, now. The proud tears were in his eyes, and he wasn't ashamed. He wiped them away without turning his head to conceal them, and swung the telescope toward a long battle line that waited in open fields below the fortified hills.

The glass hunted along the ranks. It found four small guns with their teams in the traces. They must be *his* guns, because the glass also found the old Cowpens flag, and the flag belonged to the Baltimore Brigade.

The telescope came to the next brigade in the line. For moments, Lex held it motionless. Then he turned to Captain Rutter.

"Thank you," he said. His tongue was stiff. He hadn't bothered to hide tears, a minute or two ago. But the emotion he felt, now, was young and small-boyish, and he couldn't share it with anyone. "Thank you very much." He put the glass into Rutter's hand.

"Find what you were looking for?"

"Yes. Well . . . not exactly. His back was turned, but he's wearing a sash, and he's riding my father's horse." Lex saw a chuckle beginning to tug at the captain's mouth. "I've curried that horse ever since I was ten."

"Oh. Yes . . . yes, I see."

"My gun's over there," Lex said. "The Union Artillery lost a right smart lot of men. I'd ought to go. . . ."

He stopped. Rutter had put the telescope to his eye, and his face had settled into a kind of stillness.

"Better wait," Rutter said. "I don't believe you can make it. Here. . . ." He passed the glass over.

Lex looked. The British Army was coming down the road that ran through the toe of the horseshoe. As he watched, it began to deploy. It drew a barrier of scarlet coats between Lex and the Virginia Brigade and the man who rode the horse Lex had curried every morning for four years, going now onto five.

All afternoon, the British Army marched back and forth, trying to find a weak spot in the American lines. Step for step, march and countermarch, the two brigades of Virginia and Baltimore militia matched its maneuvers. Wherever the red-coated regiments threatened to strike, they found the blue regiments waiting to meet the attack.

The attack did not come. The British Fleet came instead. After eight hours of unceasing bombardment, the five mortar ships and the *Erebus* closed in to short range.

"Now!" Rutter said softly. "Now we'll see! No, Landon —stay here. You've had your chance at them. It's our turn now." He went clattering down the lighthouse stairway, taking each flight in three jumps.

The silent fort broke its silence. McHenry erupted with the volcanic explosion of forty guns firing together. From the gun barges lying along the shore below the lighthouse, from the privateer schooners and brigs anchored behind a barricade of sunken ships in the harbor entrance, from the mud-wall batteries and the brick bastions of Fort McHenry, a storm of shot burst upon the attacking squadron.

Lex thought he saw *Erebus* hit . . . hit again . . . and again . . . and again. He thought the bomb vessels were being hurt, but he was too far away to be sure. After half an hour, the British ships turned and fled. A swarm of small boats came from the frigates to tow the battered *Erebus* out of danger.

The thunder of the American guns died away. Safely beyond their reach, the mortar ships once more opened fire.

As the smoke cloud thickened and darkened again over Fort McHenry, black storm clouds began to rise in the western sky. Out of them came the first gust of a savage wind. It stirred the great battle flag over the silent fort.

For the first time since the bombardment began, the fifteen broad stripes streamed out at full length. They blew straight and taut in the churning smoke.

The fifteen stars were the first to shine in the darkening sky.

The campfires of the two armies began to shine in the dusk. They made a half circle along the American field-works—a red, glowing horseshoe on the black anvil of hills. The British fires drew a new battle line along the side of the horseshoe nearest to Fort McHenry.

The fires gave Lex an idea. He tried to put it out of his mind. He had already done enough crazy, reckless things to last him the rest of his life. But he studied the fires a long time. There was one dark gap in the British line.

The twilight was almost gone when Captain Rutter and

Captain Herman ran up the stairs. Six or eight sailors clattered behind them and followed them out to the walkway. While they huddled around him, Rutter talked in low, earnest tones. The wind gusts blew most of his words away. But Lex heard snatches about night signals and lookouts and picket boats rowing the river to guard against a surprise attack.

The two captains, turning to leave, stopped at the railing to gaze at the gleaming fires.

"What d' you make of that British line, Wynn?"

"They're trying to fool us," the privateersman replied. "Let's hope it's themselves they fool."

"I wouldn't count on it. That's the strongest part of our front. Harris Creek runs for a mile along the foot of the hills. Deep. Steep banks."

"I know," Herman said. "They can't be big enough fools to try hitting us there. Those fires are a trick."

"The kind of trick that can work either way. They might hit us there because it's the last place we'd expect to be hit. Will you listen to those mortars! Fifteen hours . . . !" Rutter's fist pounded the rail. "They're going to try something tonight! I wish I knew what."

"We'll find out soon enough."

"Or will we find out too late?"

They hurried away.

Lex had made up his mind. If the British were going to try something tonight, he wanted to be with his father. He didn't want to listen and watch and not know what was going on.

He leaned on the rail and waited for the rain to come. The wind gusts were stronger and stronger. It was going to be a bad night. It was going to be a good night for what he intended to do.

That glimpse he'd had through the telescope of a familiar figure on a familiar horse wasn't enough. Three weeks ago, he had started out to find his father. Tonight he was going to do it.

The campfires had shown him how.

Chapter 16

DREAD SILENCE IN THE NIGHT

THE rain came. Lex took one more look at the British fires to make sure they hadn't changed. The dark gap was still there.

He was drenched to the skin when he turned away from the rail. Water ran down his legs and dripped on the stairs. He had to put his shoulder against the outer door of the lighthouse. When he got it open, the wind almost pushed him back. It was a splendid storm.

He began to walk toward the gap in the British line.

The rain didn't fall. It came toward him in sheets so solid that he could see them in spite of the dark. They bellied and flapped like linen sheets on a clothesline. Where they dragged on the ground, they made a continuous rushing sound like a stream pouring down a cascade of jumbled rocks.

Lex began to worry about the fires. He was counting on them. It was the fires that had shown him where he could slip through the British line. If the rain put them out . . .

When he got to the top of the last long ridge, the fires were still burning. They looked pushed down and flattened against the ground. The red light was penned up in small patches. Even a few feet away from the fires, the fields were invisible.

Lex went on confidently.

The ground was slippery and soft. The rain and the darkness that hid him, the wet, rushing noise of the wind and the rain that drowned out the sounds of his feet in the mud also hid the column of men marching down the slope toward the gap in the line of fires, and drowned out the sound of their marching.

Lex didn't see them or hear them. He only realized suddenly that the fire at one end of the gap had gone out. No! It hadn't gone out! He saw it in streaks between black, moving streaks of darkness. It looked like a fire behind a board fence, with wide cracks between the boards. But a fence didn't move! Lex went down on his face in the mud.

He lay there and watched the fire winking between the legs of the marching men. It gave him a strange feeling to lie there and watch those legs going steadily toward the hidden creek and the blurry red light of the American campfires on the hills beyond. It was worse than strange; it was frightening. They're going to try something tonight. The British Army was closing in for a night attack. A trick that will work either way. It was moving against the strongest part of the American line. The last place we'd expect to be hit.

The striding legs were gone. He could see the fire again.

He lay in the mud and waited and watched for more troops.

Two soldiers came out of the dark with long tree limbs clutched in their arms. They threw the wood on the fire. They stood and looked at the fire, until the dead branches began to burn. Then they disappeared.

But there were no more marching columns. Lex began to wonder. The one that had passed hadn't been the whole army. It had been too short for even a regiment. Maybe that column had been the rear guard. Maybe the British Army was already forming along the creek. Maybe it was already across, unseen in the storm and the darkness. Maybe . . .

He realized, suddenly, that there was something wrong about the fire. There were no soldiers around it! The only men he had seen were those in the column, and the two who had fetched the wood. It struck him, now, that he hadn't seen any other sign of troops in that line of fires that stretched out for a mile or more. He felt like a fool. They weren't campfires! They were a trick!

But what kind of trick?

He crawled on down the slope, through the gap, and so far beyond it that he was sure no sudden flare-up of flames could betray him. Then he got to his feet and began to work slowly along the fires.

He saw a few more men carrying armloads of wood, hauling tree limbs, or lugging whole logs between them. But by the time he came to another dark gap, he knew that the British Army was somewhere else. It certainly wasn't here.

He hadn't noticed this gap from the lighthouse walkway. It had been too far away. But there was a half mile of black dark before the red glows curved away to match the bend in the horseshoe of duller red light on the hills.

He walked toward the glows—and almost walked into another column of troops.

The column was standing still. He got only one quick glimpse of it—a darker streak in the blackness—against one of those white, flapping sheets of rain. Except for the rain, he wouldn't have seen it at all until too late. He was so close that he didn't dare throw himself down. Any sudden movement might show in those blowing white flurries.

He raised one foot carefully out of the sticky dirt and settled it firmly behind him, and lifted the other foot. One slow step at a time, he backed away from the column until he felt safe. Safer, anyway. Then he stood still, listening, watching.

The feeling of strangeness took hold again. It seemed impossible that thousands of men were standing only a few steps away, and he couldn't see them or hear them. *Thousands.* . . . For all he knew, that column might be nothing but a platoon, or a half platoon. And it might be the whole British Army.

He tried to remember the roads and the fields as he had seen them through Rutter's telescope. He hadn't been looking for roads; he hadn't cared what the fields looked like, when he was trying to pick out his father. But it seemed to him now that there had been a straight stretch of road that came down the long slant of the fields. . . .

Of course. He had seen it when Captain Rutter gave him the glass the second time to look at the British Army.

The army had been marching down a road that led straight through the toe of the fortified horseshoe of hills.

It seemed to Lex now that the road was the only place, on the whole two miles of the horseshoe, where the British hadn't threatened to make an attack this afternoon. Why? There must be some reason. Maybe the reason was that they had been saving the road for tonight.

Lex began circling back toward the column, one slow, careful step at a time. He saw it at last, and backed away, made another long circle down the slope, and found the column once more.

Back away . . . circle . . . stop. Over and over again. The motionless column seemed endless. Back away . . . another long circle. . . . Then, as he moved toward the column again, one of the fires beyond it burst into a vivid flare. Against the flames, he saw the unmistakable, glistening shapes of sailors' round, varnished hats. The naval brigade! This was the whole army. Most of it, anyway.

He backed away. He made the next circle longer. And there were still men in column, waiting, waiting—a human battering-ram more than half a mile long.

Lex pulled back. No more circling, now. He went down the slope as fast as he could drag his clumsy great lumps of feet. The ground became firmer. There was thick, matted grass. He stumbled over the stubs of small trees where the thickets along the creek had been cut away so that British troops, attacking, would have no shelter.

He neither saw nor heard the men who rose up around him. He only felt the dripping hand that closed over his mouth, and the other hands that gripped him by both arms at once.

The hands jerked him and dragged him along so fast that he lost his footing. They hauled him, then, like a sack.

He didn't know, until he heard the feet of the men beside him set the loose planks of a bridge to rattling, whether he had been caught by a British patrol or American pickets. But the bridge must carry the road over the creek, and he knew he was being taken to the American lines.

Then there was blinding light in his eyes. There was smoke hot and foul in his mouth, and stinking and hot in his nose. He saw a log gate swinging, closing behind him. Under a torch that stank and dripped burning oil, lips bristling with unshaved whiskers said, "For the love of ... A *boy!*"

"The British . . ." Lex choked on the smoke. "Their whole army's on the road. In column. They're ready to attack!"

"In column!" The bristled lips smiled. "That's likely now, isn't it? In column, all neat and handy, right under our guns."

The men holding Lex snickered. He yelled into the grinning face:

"They are! They've been there an hour! I've seen them. It's like yesterday. That column . . ."

"Oh-hoh! I see. You were in the battle." It was a way of saying he hadn't been in the battle.

"Yes, I was!"

After that, it was Captain Herman's suspicion all over again. The same questions. The names. His father's name. Captain Montgomery's. Stricker's. He shouted in desperation, "Take me to General Smith!" They snickered again at that. A voice with a rasping edge cut the snickering short:

"Captain, are you in command of this post?" A naval officer stood at the edge of the smoky light. "I'm Commodore Porter. My guns are in the batteries on this road. If what this boy says is true . . ."

"Of course it's not true!"

"Have you sent a patrol to find out?"

"We haven't got men to waste on every fool rumor. There've been too blasted many rumors! The British are planting them. They sent this boy in, like as not. But they're not sending troops in column against 130 guns."

"Only nine of which are in position to sweep that road. An assault column such as this boy describes could take the fire of nine guns and overrun them before they could be reloaded. *Have you sent a patrol?*"

The "No" came sullenly.

"Then I shall." Porter turned away. Over his shoulder, he said, "If you haven't sent that boy to General Smith in five minutes, I'll do it myself."

The captain swore, but he gave the order. The militiamen's hands hadn't let go of Lex's arms. Now they closed down hard. They hustled him up the road, past gun pits where sailors squatted over kettles in which fire glowed, and past trenches where bigger fires showed infantry huddling under makeshift roofs made of doors and odd pieces of lumber.

As they came to the top of the hill, the sound of the shells bursting over McHenry became a rumble like distant thunder. Even through the endless downpour of rain, Lex saw the fort—a volcano erupting again in great fountains of flame under a fiery cloud. He even saw the flag in the flash of a bomb that blew the top out of the cloud.

Then there were bivouac fires on both sides of the road. There were tents, and huts made of dead brush, and open-faced lean-to's, and men peering out of burrows dug into the earth, and rows of cannon with gunners holding boxes and pieces of canvas over the touchholes to keep them dry.

Then there was a larger tent, and sentries with bayonets, and officers coming and going, and one of them finally leading him into the tent. He was standing in front of a big, grizzled man with a big, fleshy face, who sat at a kitchen table. Then Lex was telling his story again. He had almost finished when Commodore Porter came in and stood dripping beside him.

"The boy's right," Porter said. "I sent a patrol, General Smith. It found them. A heavy column."

"How heavy?"

"The lieutenant who led the patrol says at least three thousand men. He isn't much given to stretching things, General. I'd say it's the bulk of their army."

General Smith began to give orders.

"To General Stricker . . . To General Winder . . . Captain Spence, this to General Forman . . ." He broke off in midsentence. His big head lifted. "What was that?"

"It's the mortars," Porter said. "I mean, sir, it's *not* the mortars. They've ceased fire."

The staff officers waiting around the table murmured among themselves. "They've quit! They're giving up! No; it could be a signal!" Smith silenced them.

"We'll continue, gentlemen, if you please." The orders went on and on. More officers hurried out.

Lex watched and listened with growing excitement. At

last, it seemed, he had done something useful. Then a young lieutenant touched his arm and beckoned him out of the tent and spoke to a sergeant standing under a dripping oak: "Keep an eye on this boy. He's to stay here until the general wants him."

"But I've got to find my father. He's . . ."

The lieutenant was already running back to the tent. Lex cried out a bitter protest:

"It isn't fair!"

"Easy, boy," the sergeant said.

"Why shouldn't I go?"

"You get to be a general, son, you'll maybe find out."

"There's no sense in standing here!"

"I dunno. I been standin' here for a week. I dunno if you win any wars that way, but your feet sure get awful sore. Glory be! Ain't it quiet! Funny—it hurts my ears. It's so still that it's louder 'n them mortar shells. I guess the Britishers must be callin' it quits."

"No," Lex said. "They aren't."

"Huh? What do you know about it?"

"I found their army. They're . . ."

"*You* found their army?" The sergeant snorted. "You sure didn't have to hunt. It's been around us all day like a swarm of red ants."

Lex kept his mouth shut after that. He had been a fool again, making brags to the sergeant because his feelings were hurt. He had got about what he deserved.

The silence went on and on. Lex felt a slow dread taking hold. It seemed to be tying a knot in his stomach.

Could this awful stillness mean that both the fleet and the army were giving up the attack? He didn't believe it. Those thousands of troops wouldn't be waiting out there in the dark, a battering-ram ready to smash the American lines, if the British intended to quit.

Could it mean that the fort had surrendered? Lex didn't believe that, either. Even if Fort McHenry had somehow been stormed and taken, the American ships would have kept on fighting, at least for a while. The firing wouldn't have stopped all at once.

Any minute, now, something would happen out there in the utter blackness that hid the road and the fort. The battering-ram would begin to move. The guns would shatter the silence into a million pieces. Minute by endless minute, Lex felt the knot of dread drawing tighter and tighter inside him. . . .

His whole body jerked. He had been waiting and listening for the same stunning roar he had heard in the afternoon—the sudden thunder of all the guns at McHenry firing at once.

But what he heard now was the faraway thump of a single cannon. The unexpected dull sound made him jump as if he never had heard a cannon before.

Another gun fired. Another. Another. But the explosions came slowly, with long aching moments of silence between them. It was as if the American cannon had been asleep and were waking up one at a time.

There was something strange going on. It seemed to Lex that the firing was not coming from the fort. Those quick red flashes that stabbed the dark were much nearer than Fort McHenry. This must be what Captain Rutter had dreaded. The British were trying something. They . . .

Fort McHenry erupted once more, and Lex understood what the British were trying to do. Their mortar ships were battering at the fort again with those terrible shells, but the guns at McHenry were not firing at the fleet. They were firing now at something behind the fort. Under cover of storm and darkness, the British had crept up the river. They were attacking McHenry now from the rear, and the fort seemed to be surrounded.

Hour after hour, Fort McHenry fought for its life in a circle of flashing guns. Hour after hour, Lex felt the earth quiver under his sopping shoes.

At last, long after midnight, the flashes changed. The guns were no longer firing toward the rear. Their quick stabs of red light began to turn until, once more, they seemed to be reaching out for the British ships. The attempt to storm the fort had failed. The Americans in the flooded trenches began to cheer.

And then, like a gallant answer, the battle flag over McHenry streamed out in the glare of the bursting bombs. The drenched soldiers cheered again.

All night, the bombs kept on coming. All night, the American Army crouched in its muddy ditches and holes, and waited for an attack that did not come.

The rain stopped at last. The first pale light in the eastern sky showed the flag still flying amid the smoke over Fort McHenry. It showed the fields, and the smoldering British fires, *and the empty road*. The British Army was gone!

The militia crawled out of the trenches. They stood on the slippery slopes of their hills, bedraggled and miserable. They were too wet and too tired to cheer when they saw the long column of the Virginia Brigade beginning to move in the sodden meadow below them, turning into the road behind the retreating British Army.

Lex had forgotten about the knot in his stomach. It had

come untied, somehow, sometime, in the night. Now it came back. It tightened around his throat, until he thought it would choke him. For there, at the head of the second regiment in the column, he saw the familiar figure—the achingly precious figure on the familiar horse.

Lex's feet moved without being told. He was down the hill and pounding over the bridge before the next regiment began to swing into the road. He was running beside the long column. His feet were dragging gobbets of mud out of the storm-soaked field and flinging them over the marching men. He was shouting his father's name.

Major Landon reined his horse off the road. He sprang down from the saddle. His arms were waiting. They held the wet, ragged, dirt-crusted boy with an incredulous, fierce relief.

"Son . . . son! Thank God. You're all right? I see you aren't, but at least you're all in one piece. Where have you been? Captain Montgomery told me that you were missing." Major Landon didn't wait for answers. His arms gripped Lex harder for just a moment, and then slid away. "A day or two, son. Then . . ."

"I'm going with you!"

"No! No, Lex, you're not! No more nonsense!" He was in the saddle again, and the horse was already trotting. "Good-by, son." He was gone.

In his haste and in his enormous relief, he had used one word that struck Lex like a blow in the face. *Nonsense.*

Chapter 17

MR. KEY BORROWS A FEATHER

Lex turned his back to the road. He couldn't stand there and watch the column go by. He'd had about all he could take.

He couldn't bear those faces leaning eagerly forward—those rows of excited, smug faces. He couldn't bear the excited chatter that came from their silly mouths.

"Got 'em on the run! We sure fixed their wagon this time! Keep 'em runnin'. You bet! Run 'em right into Chesapeake Bay!"

Those men hadn't fought. They hadn't ever been shot at. Yet they could go, and he couldn't!

Lex had never felt quite so lonely in all his life. He walked away into the field, toward the sickly smoke that rose from the burned-out fires. It was sour in his mouth, and his thoughts were as ugly and sour as the smoke.

He came to a trail of footprints, sunk deep in the mud. The ground between them was littered with lumps of mud that had dropped from his feet last night. There was one greasy chunk with his heel mark in it, as plain as the print made by a wooden stamp on a crock of butter. For all the good he had done, last night, he might just as well have been sitting in the kitchen back home with a bowl on his knees, poking and squeezing his mother's new churning with a big wooden paddle. That was about all his father thought he was able to do!

He glowered at the tracks. Then he followed them. He had nothing better to do.

The tracks surprised him a little. He hadn't circled as far away from the road as he thought he had. And he hadn't known he had gone so close to it, either, when he swung back. The last two prints, side by side, weren't three feet from the edge of the road. He had really been taking chances!

And for what? After all the commotion he'd raised, nothing had happened. Just nothing. The British had gone away.

Lex finally got tired of standing and scowling at his own footprints. Over in the meadow, the Baltimore regiments had broken ranks. Their cook fires were sending up little curls as tight as the tails of the pigs whose bacon was sizzling now on the ends of their ramrods. He supposed he could go find the Union Artillery. They'd see that he got some breakfast. But he didn't belong, and they certainly didn't need him. They likely would think he was hanging around to get his back patted for riding the gun team.

He wandered off aimlessly for a while along the black

smears of ashes and the last wisps of smoke that were left
from the British trick that had never come off. Then he
made up his mind to go back to the lighthouse. At least
it was something to do. He'd like to see what had happened to Fort McHenry.

When he came to the lighthouse, a sentry was standing
guard at the door. There hadn't been any sentry yesterday. Now that the battle was over, everything was very
proper and military. No, he couldn't come in! The sentry
was rough about it.

Lex stood at the edge of the bluff and looked across the
channel. He couldn't see much of the fort, but what he
could see was much more than he had expected. The
buildings were still there, inside, and they still had most
of their roofs. Part of a bastion wall had been blown away,
and there were black patches that looked as if the brick
parapets had been scorched by the bomb blasts. All
around the fort, the earth was torn up and churned and
pock-marked with shell holes. Burned rockets stuck in the
dirt like charred, crooked fence posts.

The whole place looked as if hogs had rooted the sod
into wallows.

The sentry finally told him to move along. Lex was too
low in his mind to care. It was just one more thing, and
one more didn't seem to matter.

He went down the zigzag path and wandered along the
shore of the harbor channel until he came to a flat ledge
that hung out over the water. The rock was warm in the
sun, and the water was deep and clear. He'd never tried
swimming with only one arm, but he guessed he could
manage. He had to tear off his sleeve to get out of his shirt.
His pants were so heavy with mud and so thoroughly plas-

tered to him that he had to sit down and crawl out of them like a crab getting rid of its shell. He dived, and hurt his arm only a little.

When he climbed out, after fifteen minutes, he felt like new. He even looked new. He couldn't get back into those filthy clothes, and the sling was as bad. So he lay on his stomach on the warm rock and hung over the edge and sloshed them and watched the dirt pouring out. When they were clean—cleaner, anyway—he spread them on bushes to dry.

He stayed there all day, in and out of the water. The sun was low when he saw a tall schooner skimming in past the lighthouse. A white gig was towing behind her.

There was something familiar about her lean, graceful lines. She rounded to in front of the barricade of sunken ships, and her sails came down with a run. He knew her then. He had seen her, with her raking masts bare, lying alongside the *Tonnant* the day he was taken aboard Admiral Cochrane's flagship. She had brought Colonel Skinner and Mr. Key to the British Fleet.

Lex scrambled into his clothes. Mr. Key was his father's friend, and on the *Surprise* he had been as kind as a man could be. He was sure Mr. Key wondered what had become of him when he disappeared from the frigate.

He saw the gig alongside the schooner now, and men stepping down from the rail. The boat pulled away, slipped through the line of anchored privateers, and came smartly up the channel. Colonel Skinner was sprawled in the stern. Mr. Key was sitting on the next thwart, his head bowed as if his big leather cap was too heavy.

Lex shouted and flourished his arm.

"Mr. Key! Mr. *Key.* . . ."

The cap came up slowly. Mr. Key's face looked haggard and white under the shiny visor. He stared a long time at the boy whose ragged clothes flapped as he danced up and down on the rock. Then he spoke to the men at the oars, and the gig shot in toward the ledge.

"Lex Landon! I'm glad to see you. I've been dreading to face your father. Get in here, Lex. Give an account of yourself."

Lex did his best as the gig pulled up the harbor. And then they were standing on a long wharf on the Baltimore waterfront, and Colonel Skinner was asking Key where he intended to stay.

"The Fountain Inn, I suppose."

"Not tonight. The Fountain had brigadier generals hanging from the chandeliers while the troops were supposed to be out in the trenches. Now half the army has come to town. Look at that street! You couldn't get into the Fountain tonight with a shoehorn."

"The Indian Queen then. Or else the barracks."

"Frank, I suppose you claim to have first call on young Landon."

"I do indeed, Colonel. I'm not letting him get away again until I see his father and get a receipt."

"Good-by, Landon." Colonel Skinner put out his hand. "You'll do! Tell your father you're going to outrank him someday. Well, Frank . . . I know you're all of an itch. I'll get along so you can start scratching. Don't worry, Landon. It isn't catching. It's an itch to write verses. So far, he's done all his scratching on one old envelope."

Skinner marched away. Key picked up his saddlebags. He and Lex had to walk single file. The footways were crowded with jubilant, jostling soldiers. The man and boy stopped once at a market stall, and Mr. Key bought bread and cheese to eat as they went along. In a little shop, he bought a packet of paper.

At the Indian Queen on Baltimore Street, there was only a bent, white-haired Negro to meet them. The owner, the clerk, the cooks, and the barman, he said, were all with the army.

"Yassuh, Lieutenant. We got a room. Ain't the best in the house, but it'll sleep you. Yassuh, help yo'self to the inkstand. Pen don't look like much, but it writes."

The pen was a gray goose quill, and the tip of the feather was broken.

The Negro led them up a dim stairway, with a brass candleholder pushed out behind him to light the steps. He opened a door, and Lex followed Mr. Key in.

Chapter 18

MR. KEY SINGS A SONG AT MIDNIGHT

THE room smelled stale. It was even smaller than Lex's own bedroom at home. It felt crowded and hot.

There was a pine bed with four posts. Somebody had worked on the posts with a jackknife. There was a small, round-topped table by one of the windows, with a straw-bottom ladder-back chair. Against one wall, an ugly black wardrobe went all the way up to the ceiling.

Only four pieces. But the room seemed to be stuffed full of furniture.

Both windows were open. The mosquito netting at one of the windows was torn.

The old Negro set the candleholder on the table and shuffled back to the door. The door closed.

Mr. Key laid the thin sheaf of paper carefully on the

table. The sheets slid and spread out a little. The candle flame made them look yellow. They lay like an ivory fan on the table.

He took the quill and the inkstand from Lex and arranged them just so. His slim hands came back to the paper. They touched it as if it were something precious. His fingertips pushed the sheets gently until they were even again, all the edges exactly together.

Then he took off his heavy cap and looked for a place to put it. There was no room on the table. He stooped and set the cap on the floor, top down, like a leather bucket. He ran his fingers quickly through the damp, matted curls of his hair.

His bloodshot eyes looked at the bed. They came back to the table, went to the bed, and came back to the table again. He shook his head slowly, wearily. Then he gave it an impatient jerk and that seemed to make up his mind.

"Go to bed, Lex. I'm going to sit up a while. I'd only lie there awake." He put one hand behind him, under the broad, short tails of his coat. The tails wagged as he fumbled at them, trying to find the pocket. "We were on the schooner these last three days—Dr. Beanes and the colonel and I—under a guard of marines. We couldn't see very much. The fort was too far away. I started writing something this morning, before we knew how the battle was going to turn out. The flag flying there in the smoke . . . Not a symbol of victory. A symbol of courage in trouble, when the outcome is still in doubt." He pulled a creased, scribbled envelope from his tail pocket. "I'd like to get it all down tonight. I don't think I can sleep till I do."

Mr. Key put the envelope on the table, at the top of the sheaf of paper. He unbuttoned his coat and hung the coat over the back of the chair. The fringe of the epaulet jiggled. It didn't shine in the candlelight. The fringe was still damp and heavy, and tarnished dull by the rain. It jiggled again as Key sat down and hitched the chair up to the table.

The battered, gray, goose-feather quill began to creak over the paper.

Lex stood by the bed and wished that he had night clothes. He didn't quite know what to do about going to bed. At least he was clean. He was glad he had taken that bath and washed out his clothes. Both the pants and the shirt were too far gone to be mended. They weren't fit for anything now, but they were clean and they had dried out right well.

Only his shoes were still wet. He sat on the floor to take them off. He wriggled out of his pants, and used the seat of the pants to make sure that his feet were clean. He slid into bed in his shirt.

The bedcords creaked. They matched the sound of the pen.

The feather bed swelled in soft bulges around him. Lex felt as if he were sinking so deep he would never come up. He wished, for a minute, that he had stayed on the floor.

This was the first time he'd been in a bed since the night he sneaked out of the house to scuttle the *Lex and Robin.* That was more than two weeks ago. He counted backward through the weeks. It was seventeen nights ago. He'd gotten out of the habit of beds and pillows. The bed was too soft. It likely would keep him awake. If it didn't, the pillow likely would smother him in his sleep.

The pen stopped. He wondered why. The pillow bulged up in front of his eyes so he couldn't see.

He wadded the pillow into a lump against the head of the bed, and looked toward the splash of yellowy candle-light on the wall. Mr. Key was sitting with his feet hooked around the legs of the chair. His face was bent over the table. His hand held the pen just over the paper, a little way down from the top of the sheet. The writing stopped there. His other hand moved. It seemed to be beating time. It made the candle flame waver.

The slow, moving hand and the flame were making Lex drowsy. His eyelids wavered. The bed was pulling him down. With his eyes half closed, he saw the hand drop to the edge of the table. Mr. Key leaned back. His face looked sick in the yellow light. His forehead and nose and chin looked as if he had taken the jaundice. The shadow that lay on the side of his face made his cheek hollow deeper.

"Lex . . . ?"

He struggled up through the warm current of sleep that was flowing over him like the Potomac.

"Are you awake, Lex?"

"Yes, sir." He didn't want to be, but he was.

"That last night . . . Tuesday night, when everything stopped. It *was* last night, wasn't it? It seems ages ago. That silence when the British stopped firing . . . Have you any idea what was going on? What their army was doing, I mean."

"Yes, sir. They were getting ready to go for us." He told how the British column was massed in the road. "Like a battering-ram. They'd picked the worst spot. The worst for us."

"What was so bad about it?"

Lex repeated what Commodore Porter had said—how an attack like that could smash things and run right over the guns.

"Did they have a good many men in the road?"

"Their whole army, almost."

"They were there a long time?"

"Yes, sir. Hours. It must have been three or four hours. They were there a long time before the mortars stopped. And afterward, too."

"All that time . . . waiting . . . thinking any minute they'd come. Is that how it was?"

"Yes, sir."

"And everything quiet?"

"You could hear the guns, when the British tried to attack the fort from behind. You could hear the bombs after that, but they were a long way off. It was right quiet, except for that."

"How did it feel? The silence? Waiting?"

"I don't know." Lex knew, but he didn't know how to say it. He remembered the slow dread tying the knot in his stomach, the knot getting bigger and harder with every minute. "It was bad, I guess." It had been worse than bad. He tried to think of another word. "It was dreadful."

"Good. That's good, Lex." Mr. Key dipped the quill in the ink. He stared at the broken end. "Army," he murmured. "Whole army . . . almost . . . host. *Host!*" The pen came down. "Silence . . . dreadful. . . ." The shabby goose feather waggled and shivered as it raced over the paper.

The candle burned crookedly. The wax dribbled down one side. It made a puddle in the brass dish, and the puddle began to harden. The wax began to run over and drip on the table.

Mr. Key glanced now and then at the scribbled envelope. The pen flew. It came at last to the end of the paper. Mr. Key laid it down. He didn't notice that it stuck in the melted wax. Or maybe it didn't matter.

He let his hands drop at his sides. He let his breath out in a long, tired sigh.

"Well . . ." He looked toward the bed. "Still awake?"

"Yes, sir."

"I've finished the verses. A fine way to spend a night." He seemed amused at himself. "They were in my head. I had to get shut of them somehow." His hand reached out for the close-written sheet. "I wrote some other verses to an old tune, a few years ago. Ten years ago—1804— when Stephen Decatur came back from the Barbary war. The tune was a song called 'To Anacreon in Heaven.' These new verses fit it, too."

He began to hum to himself. His head nodded, keeping time, and his hand began to keep time. Then he pushed back the chair and stood up, still humming, and walked to the door. There was room for only four steps. He turned and walked to the table and turned and walked back again. As he walked, he began to sing. His voice was so low that Lex heard the opening words only faintly. . . .

O say, can you see, by the dawn's early light,
    What so proudly we hail'd. . . .

Lex felt a quick twinge of shame. He hadn't been proud, in the sickly pale dawn this morning. He had been sulky and hurt and sullen, because his father would not

let him go with the army, and didn't have time to listen,
and nobody knew nor cared about what he had done.

Mr. Key's voice was rising now. It was vibrant and
clear.

> Whose broad stripes and bright stars
>   through the perilous fight, . . .

Lex had seen the broad stripes blowing out through
the driving smoke. He had seen the stars shine when the
sky had no other stars.

He hadn't been in that perilous fight. He had only
looked on. But he had been in another fight, and somehow the words Mr. Key was singing made him think of
General Stricker's big, sun-scalded nose glowing like a
red-hot coal in his face, and his whole face glowing with
pride in his men. Not in himself, but his men. Now, for
the first time, Lex began to see how wrong he had been in
his own touchy pride.

> And the rocket's red glare, the bomb bursting in air,
> Gave proof through the night that our flag was still
>   there: . . .

He hadn't thought of the bombs and the rockets that
way. He had found a different kind of proof when he
looked through a borrowed telescope at the great horseshoe of trenches and guns, and saw them as proof of a
power and a strength that would always keep the flag of
his country safe.

> Where the foe's haughty host in dread silence reposes, . . .

That was his line! The wind and the rain and the
silence. The long column, waiting and deadly. That was

Lex Landon's line, and he was a part of the song. It didn't matter now that the attack never came and his warning had gone for nothing. It didn't matter if nobody ever knew what he had tried to do. He had been a part of something important—the something that made Mr. Key's voice tremble and come near to breaking now.

> O! thus be it ever, when freemen shall stand
> Between their lov'd home and the war's
> desolation! . . .

He had seen them standing . . . the men at the three little guns . . . the other gun smashed in the road . . . and the smashed bodies in the road. The bayonets coming. The bayonets only ten steps away. The gunners . . . the few who were left . . . standing bravely in their places to fire the last possible shot . . . and then charging a British regiment . . . five men fighting five hundred with rammers and naked hands and their naked courage.

He had seen them standing . . . the tired, dirty, beaten men . . . the men who ran from an army three times as strong . . . and stopped running . . . and turned . . . and stood waiting to fight again. The men who conquered the fears of their shaking bodies . . . and made their bodies a living rampart to guard their homes and their country.

Mr. Key was coming toward him now. He was smiling as he sang. He was holding out the paper. Lex sat up to take it. A few of the words were crossed out. The last few lines were squeezed close together. They seemed to be crowding each other, trying to stay on the page. Mr. Key's slim finger was tapping the paper, pointing, touching the last two lines. He was looking at Lex, and there seemed

to be something he wanted. He was lifting his hand . . .
reaching . . . wanting to lift something out of Lex Landon.

Frank Key's head went back. His bloodshot eyes closed,
and his face was gaunted and white.

Lex nodded. He didn't know why. Mr. Key couldn't
see the nod. Lex took a deep breath and let Mr. Key's
words come. . . .

And the star-spangled banner in triumph doth wave
O'er the land of the free and the home of the brave.

Mr. Key stood for a moment with his face lifted to
something he seemed to see behind the closed lids of his
eyes.

Then he smiled and reached for the verses. He walked
to the table and put them down. His fingers began to
undo the white band at his neck.

"Good night, Lex."

"Good night, Mr. Key."

He ought to say something about the song. He ought
to say how he felt. He couldn't. The feeling was too deep
inside him.

He slid his legs down. He burrowed his hipbone into
the bed, trying to make it solid. He hadn't slept in a bed
for so long. . . . He'd forgotten how long. He was too
tired to count back again.

Tomorrow or next day, he'd be with his father, and his
father would have time to talk.

They'd have plenty to talk about. It would last them
all the way home.